Oops!

TJ and the TIME STUMBLERS

BOOK 3
Oops!

Bill Myers

Tyndale House Publishers, Inc.
Carol Stream, Illinois

Visit Tyndale's exciting Web site for kids at www.tyndale.com/kids.

Visit Bill Myers's Web site at www.billmyers.com.

TYNDALE and Tyndale's quill logo are registered trademarks of Tyndale House Publishers, Inc.

Oops!

Designed by Stephen Vosloo

Edited by Sarah Mason

Published in association with the literary agency of Alive Communications, Inc., 7680 Goddard Street, Suite 200, Colorado Springs, CO 80920, www.alivecommunications.com.

This novel is a work of fiction. Names, characters, places, and incidents either are the product of the author's imagination or are used fictitiously. Any resemblance to actual events, locales, organizations, or persons living or dead is entirely coincidental and beyond the intent of either the author or the publisher.

For manufacturing information regarding this product, please call 1-800-323-9400.

Library of Congress Cataloging-in-Publication Data

Myers, Bill, date.
  Oops! / Bill Myers.
     p. cm. — (TJ and the time stumblers ; bk. 3)
     Summary: In training to become a future world leader, Malibu Junior High School student TJ continues her mishaps with her "helpers" from the twenty-third century, who have provided her with a Thought Broadcaster Pen that forces her to try to stop returning meanness to those who are mean to her.
     ISBN 978-1-4143-3455-4 (sc)
  [1. Conduct of life—Fiction. 2. Christian life—Fiction. 3. Time travel—Fiction.
4. Junior high schools—Fiction. 5. Schools—Fiction. 6. Malibu (Calif.)—Fiction.]
I. Title.
  PZ7.M98234Oo 2011
  [Fic]—dc23   2011015994

Printed in the United States of America

17   16   15   14   13   12   11

 7   6   5   4   3   2   1

For Grant Gonzalez: friend, fellow learner,
and pond cleaner extraordinaire!

CHAPTER ONE

Beginnings . . .

TIME TRAVEL LOG:
Malibu, California, November 2

Begin Transmission:
All-school bully from the future stopped by. Despite
his disguise, Tuna and I are positive it's Bruce
Bruiseabone, winner of the Worst Breath in the
World Contest. We fear he could really zwork things
up for our subject (who, by the way, is still smoot to
the max).

End Transmission

Thelma Jean Finkelstein, better known as TJ to her
friends (all four of them—unless you leave out her

goldfish and pet hamster, which brings it down to two friends), ran through the empty cafeteria, screaming her lungs out.

"AᴴHʜHHʜʜ!"

And when she wasn't

"AᴴHʜHHʜʜ!"-ing

she was yelling,

"Why is he chasing us?
Why is he chasing us?!"

Now, you might call her behavior a little weird (which may be why she has only two friends). But weirder than that weirdness is that the **HE** in her little screamfest just happened to be an African elephant the size of a Chevy pickup who, unlike a Chevy pickup, had some very bad breath.

Weirder than *that* weirdness was that the African elephant (complete with large tusks and a crummy mood) was shouting in a very bad British accent,

"Excuse me, miss. If you don't mind, I should like to speak with you a moment!"

Weirder than *that* weird weirdness was the *US* TJ happened to be screaming about. And who, exactly, was the *US*?

Actually, they were nobody. (Unless you counted the two invisible teenagers from the 23rd century who were running beside her.)

First, there was Thomas Uriah Norman Alphonso the Third. Or for those who don't enjoy spraining their tongues, Tuna. On TJ's other side ran Herby, a tall surfer dude with long blond bangs and the exact same number of brain cells as TJ had friends (*after* you subtract the goldfish and hamster).

The boys had traveled back in time to do a history report on TJ because, believe it or not, someday when she was through screaming her lungs out and being chased by African elephants through school cafeterias, TJ would become a great world leader.

But until then, she had other things on her mind like

"*AHHHHHH!*

Get us out of here!

Get us out of here!"

"No worries, Your Dude-ness," Herby shouted. "I'll transport us home!" With that he pulled out his trusty Swiss Army Knife (sold at 23rd-century time-travel stores everywhere), opened its Transporter Beam Blade, and

chugga-chugga-chugga

BLING!

The good news was Herby transported them out of the cafeteria.

The bad news was he missed TJ's house (unless she had moved to the top of Mount Everest).

The top of Mount Everest! you say?

Yeah, that's what TJ was saying too. Only more like

"THE TOP OF MOUNT EVEREST!"

"How odd!" Tuna yelled over the howling wind.

"That we're on Mount Everest?" Herby shouted. "Or that the elephant is still behind us?"

"Actually, I'm talking about the end of the giant glacier we're approaching."

"What end?" Herby shouted. "What glacier?"

"The end we've just reached and the glacier we are now jumping

O
F
F
F
F
F
F
!
!
!"

Wanting to be part of the conversation, TJ threw in her own comment—the always clever and very appropriate

"A

H

H

H

H

H

H

!

!

!"

And refusing to be left out, the elephant, who was falling beside them, added,

"I

d

o

believe

this

may

hurt

a

b

i

t

!"

But thanks to Herby's great thinking (and accidental good luck), he tried the Transporter Beam Blade
again and

chugga-chugga-chugga

instead of hitting the ground, they

BLING!-ed

back to school and were running down the hallway
toward the auditorium.

That was the good news. But as you may recall,
every time TJ gets a little good news, she gets a
ton of bad. In this case, it came in the form of one

African elephant (whose breath had not improved) who was still running after them. And (since we're having a two-for-one special in TJ's bad luck department) there was the added problem of Hesper Breakahart, star of her own TV series on the Dizzy Channel (and the richest, most gorgeous, most spoiled 13-year-old in the entire civilized world— and maybe Texas, too). At the moment she was inside that very auditorium holding auditions for her TV show.

* * * * *

"Now remember, kiddies," the TV director with a bad hairpiece said to nearly a hundred girls sitting in the auditorium, "we're looking for somebody to play Hesper's younger sister. It's going to be tough. You might have to memorize lines, remember where to move, and—" he lowered his voice—"the people in wardrobe may even want you to wear glasses."

All the wannabe actresses shuddered. "Eeew . . ."

"I know; I know," the director agreed. "Acting can be brutal. But it's the price one pays for stardom. Isn't that right, Ms. Breakahart?"

"That's right," Hesper said, flashing her perfect, glow-in-the-dark, bleach-toothed smile.

All the girls grinned, flashing their own perfect, glow-in-the-dark smiles. (Malibu Junior High girls have a thing about perfect, glow-in-the-dark smiles. They also have a thing about perfect skin, perfect tans, and perfect anything else their rich mommies and daddies can afford.)

The director turned to Hesper. "So, Ms. Breakahart, who would you like to audition first?"

Every little-sister hopeful's hand shot up like they all had to go to the bathroom.

"*oh! Oh! oh!*"

"*Please Please! Please*"

"*Me! Me! Me!*"

Chad Steel glanced up from the homework he was doing at the back of the auditorium. Earlier, Hesper had asked him to swing by and give her some emotional support. It seemed Hesper always needed his emotional support. And since they were supposed to be "a couple" and since Chad was the nicest guy in school, he helped her out when he could.

At the moment "helping out" meant watching Hesper audition her fellow students for a tiny part in her TV series. Lately, she'd been making so many enemies (courtesy of the New Kid) that Hesper figured this would be a great way to play kissy-kissy to everyone.

And it seemed to be working.

Even Miss Grumpaton, their fossilized English teacher, was there. "I could play her *slightly* older sister," she said. (I guess even old people have fantasies.)

But Mr. Beaker, the science teacher, had definitely gone too far. Honestly, who did the guy think he was fooling by wearing that wig and miniskirt?

The point is, *everyone* wanted to be a star. Which meant they were all slaves to Hesper Breakahart's slightest whim.

"Let's see," Hesper said, tossing her perfect blonde hair held in place by 4½ cans of hair spray (and one full-time hairstylist). "How about . . . you!"

"Me?" A shorter version of Hesper leaped to her feet. "Really? Really, really?!"

"Yes, uh . . . what is your name?"

"Elizabeth."

Hesper frowned.

"You know, Elizabeth Mindlessfan. I've been your best friend since forever?"

"Oh yes, of course. Well, go up on the stage, uh . . . um . . ."

"Elizabeth," Elizabeth said.

"Right. Go up there and read the lines."

"Oh, goody," Elizabeth squealed as she raced to the stage and took her place. "Goody, goody, goody!"

"Are you ready?" the director asked.

"Oh yes! Absolutely, yes, yes, yes!"

"All right, then," the director said. "And . . . action!"

Elizabeth looked down at the script in her hands and read, "Oh, Hesper, you're so beautiful and talented and beautiful and rich and did I mention beautiful?" (If you'd guessed Hesper helped write the script, you'd have guessed right.) "I hope that some- day I'll grow up to be just as beautiful and talented and beautiful and rich and—did I mention beauti- ful?—as you."

"And cut!" the director shouted. "That was won- derful, babe. You're a natural."

"Really?" Elizabeth squealed in delight.

"You bet," he said. "You were magic."

"Goody, goody, goody!"

Chad looked down, shaking his head. It was amazing how crazy people got when they thought

they could be on TV. He was about to return to
his work when the auditorium door suddenly flew
open and

"AHHHHHH!"

one very loud and very frightened New Kid ran in.

To be honest, Chad wasn't entirely surprised.
It seemed the New Kid was always doing unusual
things—which in a strange way he found kinda cute.
Not that he had a thing for escaped mental patients,
but ever since she moved in next door to him, there'd
been something about her he found . . . interesting.

And this was the perfect example. Because not
only was she running down the aisle toward the front
exit yelling,

"Why is he still chasing us?

Why is he still chasing us?!"

but as far as Chad could tell, there was no **US** being
chased. It was just the New Kid. But even more
interesting was the fact that she was being chased
down the aisle by an African elephant.

Naturally, everyone screamed and panicked. And those girls who had been raising their hands like they had to go to the bathroom? Well, this time it was for real (and it might have been too late).

Without thinking, Chad leaped to his feet and ran toward the New Kid and her peanut-eating pet. He wasn't sure why. Maybe he thought even mental patients deserved protection from runaway elephants. Whatever the reason, he'd read that the best way to handle wild animals was to stand up to them and not be afraid. This would explain his running down the aisle, waving his arms, and screaming like a madman. Either that or he'd caught whatever mental disorder the New Kid had.

Still, it did not explain why the elephant stopped, turned on its heels (or paws or whatever elephants turn on), and said in a very poor English accent,

"Excuse me. You needn't be rude."

Chad's jaw dropped—either because the elephant spoke or because Chad had never been accused of being rude. (Though if he'd really wanted to be mean, he could have said something about the animal's breath.)

In any case, the elephant continued speaking.

"I merely wish to warn the young lady about the DANGERS of allowing these two invisible boys floating beside—"

He would have said more, but he was interrupted by the New Kid screaming,

"Herby! Tuna! DO someth—"

And she would have said more, except it's hard saying more when you suddenly

chugga-chugga-chugga

BLING!

disappear.

Instantly, everything was back to normal—well, except for those girls racing to the bathroom . . . and the lingering bad breath of an African elephant who had just vanished from everyone's sight.

CHAPTER TWO

Pass the Underwear, Please

TIME TRAVEL LOG:
Malibu, California, November 2–supplemental

Begin Transmission
Subject may be questioning our motives. As if we really want to be stuck in the 21st century, where kids not only have to brush their teeth but floss them (which sometimes leaves little white flecks on their mirrors). GROSS!

End Transmission

TJ stood at the table, helping Violet, her middle sister, fold laundry. It was one of the things Mom did for them before she died of cancer almost a year ago. And one of the gazillion memories that always made TJ's heart hurt. Of course there were other memories. Little things like Mom

—always listening to TJ when she needed to talk
—always holding TJ when she needed to cry
—always forgiving TJ when she'd been a brat

and plenty more. They always came to mind when TJ didn't expect them. And they made her eyes water and her throat ache at the weirdest of times.

Dad did his best to fill in. But Dad was . . . well, Dad was a dad. At the beginning he tried to do everything himself. You know, things like

FIXING MEALS—But after a steady diet of semifrozen hot dogs, semifrozen pizza (Dad never got the hang of using the microwave), and semifrozen hot chocolate (don't even ask), the girls decided to take over.

Then there was

CLEANING HOUSE—He'd seen people using vacuum cleaners on TV. He just wasn't sure how to turn it on. And who knew what type of green mold he was growing in the sinks and inside the shower stall.

Then there was

DOING LAUNDRY—Let's face it: there's something just plain wrong with a dad sorting your underwear.

Not that sorting it in front of two teenage boys from the 23rd century was much better. But that was nothing compared to the embarrassment of being chased through the auditorium this afternoon by an elephant. And what was his warning about Tuna and Herby? Not that she put much trust in stampeding African elephants, but still . . .

"Actually, it was Bruce Bruiseabone disguised as an African elephant," Tuna whispered. He was floating, cross-legged, beside her.

TJ frowned, making it clear she didn't want her sister to hear his voice and freak out.

"That's right, Your Dude-ness," Herby whispered from the other side. "Bruce is like our all-school bully. He was just torking with you. By the way, is that *really* what 21st-century people wear under their clothes?"

It was Herby's turn to be frowned at.

Tuna continued. "Ever since Herby accidentally blew up Bruce's locker with a neutron bomb from science class, the guy has had this thing against him."

Herby nodded. "Some people are so sensitive."

TJ threw a nervous look to her sister and whispered, "Not now, guys . . . but we definitely need to talk."

Violet looked up. "What's that?"

TJ cleared her throat. "I said, I'll, uh, definitely need some socks."

Violet shoved the pile at her. "Knock yourself out. The sooner I get out of here, the better."

Violet wasn't being rude (well, no ruder than usual). She just had a lot of other things to do. As a brilliant overachiever, she always had other things to do. If it wasn't finishing up a report that wasn't due for another 10 weeks, it was reading another seven or eight books by morning. Then there was the whole world hunger thing to solve. But, hey, the night was young.

"So," Violet asked as she smoothed the wrinkles from one of Dad's shirts, "what about this elephant?"

TJ groaned. "You guys heard about it in the elementary school, too?"

"Everybody's heard about it," Violet said. "Where exactly do you think it came from?"

"It was Bruce Bruiseabone," Tuna sighed. "How many times do you have to be told?"

"What's that?" Violet asked.

TJ coughed. "How many times do we have to fold? These socks, I mean? I forget."

Violet gave her a look, then slowly answered, "We fold them like we always fold them."

Uh-oh, her sister was definitely getting suspicious. TJ had to throw her off track, try something new, something she'd never attempted before. She had it! She'd pretend to like her.

"Isn't this just great?" TJ grinned. "You and me working together like this?" She could feel Violet eyeing her and added, "I just love doing laundry, don't you?"

"Uh, no. And neither do you."

"Oh . . . well." TJ giggled, "Hee-hee-hee." And then, with no other plan, she grinned bigger and threw in another "Hee-hee-hee."

Violet stared at her.

TJ grinned even bigger.

Violet continued staring.

TJ continued grinning . . . though the corners of her mouth had started to droop.

Finally Violet repeated the question. "What about that elephant?"

"Oh, I don't know." TJ shrugged as she reached for another sock. "Probably came from Hesper Breakahart's private zoo or something. The spoiled creep has everything else."

"You shouldn't say that about her," Violet said.

"That's right," Herby agreed. "She doesn't have a zoo."

"What's that?" Violet asked.

TJ coughed. "I said she can be so rude."

"Just the same, you know how Dad hates it when we talk trash about people."

"The dude obviously doesn't know Bruce Bruiseabone," Herby said more loudly.

"Herby!" TJ whispered.

"What did you say?" Violet asked.

But Herby wasn't finished. "He is zworked beyond the max, and if you ask me—"

TJ tried covering his voice by humming. *"Hummm . . . hummm . . . hummm."* (All right, it wasn't her best idea, but it was sure a lot better than the one she'd have in chapter nine.)

Violet looked at her suspiciously.

TJ just smiled and continued to, *"Hummm . . . hummm . . . hummm."*

Which meant Tuna had to raise his voice when he asked, **"What are you doing?"**

TJ hummed louder. *"Hummm . . . hummm . . . hummm."*

Violet continued to frown.

"I think she's humming!" Herby shouted to Tuna.

Violet's eyes darted around the room. "Who said that?"

"Hummm . . . hummm . . . hummm."

"I didn't hear you!" Tuna yelled. *"What is she doing?"*

"Hummm . . . hummm . . . hummm."

"She's humming!!"

"Hummm . . . hummm . . . hummm."

"Oh!"

The good news was the boys had finally figured out the humming question.

The bad news was TJ was humming so loud she couldn't get enough air and was hyperventilating.

The worse news was that when people run out of air and hyperventilate, they have a tendency to

THUD

pass out.

* * * * *

Trent Tauntalot, a hulking ninth grader, faked to the left, spun to the right, and fired the ball to Chad

Steel, who caught it in midair and laid it up, bringing the score to 19–19.

"All right!" Scott, the other teammate, shouted.

"That's what I'm talkin' about!" Trent yelled as the three boys high-fived. "Let's bury 'em! Let's clean the court with 'em! Let's make 'em sorry they ever lived!"

You may have noticed, Trent liked winning. Actually, he didn't like winning as much as he hated losing. Because losing was, well, for losers. And Trent Tauntalot was no loser. He was a man. And someday his voice would change to prove it (he hoped).

"Defense!" Trent shouted. "Full-court press!"

The three boys headed down the outdoor court and stayed glued to their men. It was getting late. The sun was setting and the fog was already rolling in from the ocean, so they were playing to sudden death. The first team to 20 would win.

"No mistakes, now!" Trent shouted. "No mistakes!"

Chad raced downcourt with Trent and Scott. Although surfing was more his thing, it felt good shooting hoops at the beach courts with the guys. It helped clear his mind. And after the wild animal safari in the auditorium this afternoon, there was a lot to clear.

"Pick him up!" Trent shouted at Chad. Somehow

Chad's man had slipped past him and was breaking for the basket. "Pick him up! Pick him up!"

Scott peeled off his own man to check Chad's. It was close, but Scott managed to get in position and stop the fast break. The opposing team of seventh and eighth graders had to take their place around the key and start passing the ball, working it in, looking for an opening.

"Come on, Steel," Trent shouted at Chad. "Get your head in the game!"

But Chad's head wasn't in the game. It was still in the auditorium. And on the New Kid. Where had that elephant come from? There was no circus in town. None had escaped from the zoo. And what about that corny British accent? Was the New Kid some kind of ventriloquist?

"Steel!"

Chad looked up just in time to see a screen had been set and his man was breaking past him with the ball. Trent rolled off to check the guy, but Chad was too late to pick up Trent's man, who was inside and open. The ball was flipped to the kid and he went in for an easy layup.

Final score: 20–19. Chad's team had lost. More importantly, Trent's team had lost (which, you may have guessed, can't be good). Knuckle bumps and high fives were shared all around . . . except by Trent. Chad had barely leaned over to catch his breath before the big guy was in his face.

"What were you thinking, man? We could have had that game!"

"Sorry," Chad said.

"'Sorry'? That's it? You're sorry?" To say Trent hated losing was an understatement. To say he'd sell his grandmother's soul to win—or at least her house, furniture, and bed (with her still in it)—was more accurate.

"Hey, take it easy," Scott said, coming to Chad's defense. "It's just a friendly game."

"There's no such thing as a friendly game!" Trent shouted. "You embarrassed me, Steel. And nobody embarrasses me."

"Except you," Scott muttered.

"What's that?"

Now Scott was no fool. Like Chad, he was only a seventh grader and half Trent's size. To avoid any broken body parts, he simply shook his head. "Forget it, man."

But Trent wouldn't forget it. That would require having class and style, and neither were Trent's specialty. He turned to Chad and yelled, "Maybe you should go home to your beauty queen movie star! Maybe you're only good at being her boy toy!"

Chad let the comment go. Everybody knew Trent was a hothead.

"Or hanging out with that new freako neighbor of yours."

Chad's head jerked up. "Hey, watch your mouth."

"What did you say?" Trent demanded.

Surprised at himself, Chad brought it down a notch. "Look, I know she's a little weird, and weird stuff keeps happening around her. But c'mon, her mom died and she just moved here from Missouri. Cut her some slack."

"The chick should be locked up with all the other sicko freaks."

Before he knew it, Chad was in Trent's face. "I said watch it!"

At which point Trent had three options:

OPTION A: Start a fight.
OPTION B: Start a fight.
OPTION C: All of the above.

So after carefully studying his options, Trent chose to push Chad away. Hard. Real hard. "What are you going to do about it, huh?"

"Guys," Scott warned.

Chad swallowed his anger. Unlike Trent, he didn't believe in fighting.

But Trent wouldn't stop. "Huh?" He gave Chad another push. "Huh?"

Chad knew walking away was the best choice—particularly when the guy outweighed him by 30 pounds. But then Trent crossed the line:

"That little psycho of yours is a freak and everyone—"

Before he could stop himself, Chad slammed his hands into Trent's chest, pushing him back.

"Chad!" Scott warned.

"Yeah." Trent broke into a sneering grin. "Bring it on!"

Chad was about to push again, until he saw Trent leaning back to throw a fist into his face. But being 30 pounds lighter also meant being 30 pounds faster, so Chad was able to dodge the blow. After the big kid finished his swing and was off-balance, Chad did the unthinkable. He hit Trent hard in the gut.

Trent gasped, grabbing his stomach. It was only one punch, but it dropped the big guy to his knees.

Chad moved in, preparing to give Trent a little free orthodontist work, but Scott grabbed him by the arm and shouted, "What are you doing? Chad, are you nuts? Chad!"

Chad blinked, coming to. What *had* he done? He looked down to Trent, who was still testing his stomach. "Hey, I'm sorry, man," Chad said. He offered his hand, but Trent ignored it. He tried again. "I don't know what I was thinking, but—"

Trent batted it away.

"Look," Scott said, stepping between them, "everyone needs to chill. Chad, maybe you should grab your stuff and head on home—cool down a bit."

Chad glanced around. Everybody on the court stood staring at him. "Yeah." He swallowed. "I, uh . . . yeah." Shaking his head over his actions, he crossed the court and grabbed his sweatshirt. He said good night to the guys and headed up the beach toward his house.

"Sure, run away!" Trent shouted. "Why don't you come back here and fight like a man?" Of course Trent might have been more convincing if he could have stood up.

Chad didn't bother to answer. He had other things on his mind . . . like how his new next-door neighbor could have fogged up his thinking like that. Weird. Very weird. He glanced at their two houses crammed side by side (all beach houses are crammed side by side). The orange glow from the setting sun reflected off their windows. And suddenly he had another question . . .

What was Elizabeth Mindlessfan, Hesper's best friend since forever, doing climbing up to the New Kid's window?

CHAPTER THREE

An Early Evening Chat

TIME TRAVEL LOG:

Malibu, California, November 2—supplemental

Begin Transmission

Must convince subject we are the good guys.
You'd think my dashing good looks, incredible
intelligence, and awesome humility would be enough.
21st-century babes can be stubborn to the max.

End Transmission

TJ paced back and forth in her bedroom. She was
having another argument with Tuna and Herby, while
trying to ignore her phone, which vibrated every

other second. It seemed half the school wanted to know what had happened with the elephant.

(The other half wanted to know what planet she was visiting from and when the mother ship was beaming her up.)

She'd love to give them an answer. Any answer. The problem was she had no answer . . . except for the boys' lame excuse about some bully from the 23rd century.

"Trust me, Your Dude-ness," Herby said. He floated cross-legged above her desk. "Bruce Bruiseabone has just come here from our century to torment us."

"You don't think he could take you home?" TJ asked as she swatted at a passing fly.

"Only if he first gets to rearrange our facial parts. The guy is majorly unsafe."

TJ frowned. "But he said *you* were the dangerous ones."

Across the room, Tuna cleared his throat. Actually, he cleared his gills, since he'd morphed himself into a goldfish and was taking several laps around TJ's fishbowl with her other fish. (Hey, it's way cheaper than going to the gym.) Earlier, Herby had hit Tuna with a beam from the Acme Thought Broadcaster so he could broadcast his thoughts through TJ's stereo speakers—much easier than interpreting all those bothersome *bubble-bubble* sounds.

"Bruce wants to ruin our reputation with you," Tuna thought, *"so our history report on you fails."*

Herby agreed. "The dude's a real pain in the doo-wa."

"Now, Herby," Tuna thought, *"just because he speaks badly about us doesn't mean we should do the same about him."*

"The guy is majorly zworked."

"Zworked or not, we should think the best of him."

TJ rolled her eyes. "You sound like my dad."

"Actually, parents are correct 94.6 percent of the time."

TJ smirked. "You sure that's not 94.5 percent?"

"When I get out and towel off, I'll double-check my figures."

Once again TJ rolled her eyes and once again TJ swatted at the buzzing fly. "But how do I know if you guys are the ones telling the truth? What if it's really this Bruce guy?"

"Obviously, because our breath smells way better."

"And we're mega-times better looking," Herby said, sucking in his stomach and checking out his reflection in the mirror. "And way more, uh, what's that word again, Tuna?"

"Intelligent."

"Right, intelligent."

Tuna stopped swimming and raised a flipper. *"Shh,"* he thought. *"Did you hear that?"*

"Hear what?" TJ asked.

"That buzzing sound."

"It's just this stupid fly," TJ said, waving it away.

"A fly?" Herby asked. He looked suspiciously over to Tuna in the fishbowl.

Tuna swished his tail nervously. *"Maybe it is . . . and maybe it isn't."*

Ever so quietly, Herby reached for his handy-dandy Swiss Army Knife.

"What's up?" TJ asked.

"It's right there on the chair," Tuna quietly thought.

"Guys?"

"I see it," Herby whispered as he slowly opened up the Stun Blade. "It may *look* like an ordinary fly . . ."

"But in reality, it's–"

Suddenly both boys yelled (or thought),

"Bruce Bruiseabone!" as Herby aimed the blade and

Wibba-Wibba-Wibba

ZOoooING!

fired at the fly. Unfortunately,

Wibba-Wibba-Wibba

ZOoooING!

is not the sound of a Stun Blade. So instead of stunning the fly or hearing a stupid buzzing sound, they now heard,

"I can hardly wait to get home to all my little maggot babies and—"

"You have activated the Translator Blade!" Tuna thought.

"—read them a bedtime story about 'Little Red Flying Gnat and the Big Bad Bug Zapper.' No, that's too scary. How 'bout 'Snow Fly and the Seven Cans of Raid'? No, no, that's even worse. Let's see—"

"It's the right blade!" Herby yelled. "It's just

shorting out." Immediately he practiced what he'd learned in six years of electronics school and

thwack-thwack-thwack-ed

it hard against the desk until

ramma ... lamma ... ding—

BLAM!

he blew up the chair. And we're not talking little bits of wood scattered here and there. We're talking . . .

"HERBY!" TJ cried. "MY CHAIR IS A PILE OF DUST!"

"Wow, glad I left the chair. I'll just buzz over to this nice dresser and—"

ramma ... lamma ... ding—

BLAM!

"THAT WAS MY DRESSER!"

"How rude! Well, I'm just going to buzz to this nice fishbowl and—"

ramma . . . lamma . . . ding—

BLAM!

(glug-glug-glug

glug-glug-glug)

"Fine. I can tell when I'm not wanted. I'm leaving through this open window to bury my sorrows in that nice mound of doggy doo-doo I saw in the yard."

All this as TJ was busy shouting, "LOOK WHAT YOU'VE DONE TO MY ROOM!"

"I was only trying to stop Bruce," Herby explained.

"*Uh, Herby?*" Tuna thought.

TJ looked all around until she spotted Tuna flopping on the floor.

"Yeah, Tuna," Herby said.

"*Would you mind morphing me back? It has become rather difficult to breathe.*"

"Oh, sure, dude." Herby opened another blade and

Krinkle . . . Krackle

PooF!

Tuna turned into a porcupine.

"*Uh, no, not exactly,*" Tuna thought.

"Sorry, this thing keeps shorting out." Herby tried again.

Krinkle . . . Krackle

PooF!

Now Tuna was a bathroom toilet, complete with a cute, furry pink cover on his lid.

"*Don't think so, Herb.*"

Krinkle . . . Krackle

PooF!

Finally the real Tuna appeared, dripping wet and wearing his silvery time-travel suit.

"We might have made a mistake," he said as he rose to his feet. "After careful consideration, I don't believe that was Bruce Bruiseabone but an actual fly."

"How do you know, dude?" Herby asked.

"Could you smell its breath?"

"No."

"My point exactly." As he spoke, Tuna stooped down and picked up the other goldfish, who was still flopping on the floor. Speaking directly to the fish, he said, "Sorry, George; we'll chat later."

"George?" TJ asked. "Her name is Gertrude."

"Actually, she's a he," Tuna said, stroking the goldfish's tiny head. "And thanks to your misnaming him, there is no telling how many years of therapy he'll need before he can lead a normal—"

"We've got company!" Herby shouted.

TJ spun around to see him aiming the blade at a girl crouching on her windowsill, videotaping them. A girl who looked exactly like . . .

"Elizabeth Mindlessfan!" TJ shouted. "Herby, don't shoot. That's Elizabeth Mindlessfan!"

TJ raced to the open window, then paused to collect herself. Finally, as calmly as possible, she said, "Well, hello there, Elizabeth. Nice of you to stop by.

Wasn't the front door working?" She offered her hand to help Elizabeth in through the window.

Elizabeth looked a little pale. Actually, she looked a lot pale—though it was hard to notice with all her sweating, shaking, and nervous twitching. Since she was busted for spying and had no other choice, she reluctantly took TJ's hand and climbed inside.

Unfortunately, this wasn't Elizabeth's first encounter with TJ and her invisible sidekicks. Besides the disappearing elephant routine, she'd seen a few other things like

—a *Treasure Island* character trapped inside TJ's locker

—a floating milk carton dumped all over Hesper Breakahart

—a bouncing Ford pickup truck with blinking Tuna eyes

Then there was the time she walked backward up TJ's wall and across her ceiling (which, of course, can only happen if you're struck by a Reverse Beam from a 23rd-century Swiss Army Knife).

No one bothered explaining any of this to her. And when she tried telling her friends, no one believed her. This would explain the video camera

in her hands. It would also explain the outfit she
wore whenever she visited TJ. A bold fashion state-
ment consisting of

> —orange coveralls, black rubber boots, and
> surgical gloves (in case TJ was a zombie ready to
> attack)
> —a hat with a bee net draped over her face
> (in case TJ was an outer space alien ready to
> hypnotize her with deadly photon rays)
> —a clove of garlic and a giant crucifix (in case
> TJ was simply your boring, run-of-the-mill vampire)

"So you've come to spy on me again?" TJ asked.
"Me?" Elizabeth croaked. "Oh no, TB." (She never
got TJ's name right.) "I was just in the neighborhood
and thought I'd stop by."
"With a video camera?"
She stared at her hand and pretended to be surprised. "Wow, how did that get there?" (She was as
bad a liar as she was a dresser.)
Suddenly the camera was yanked from her hands
and floated across the room to where it hovered
over the desk. Elizabeth wanted to scream, but
it's hard screaming when you're about to pass out
from fear.

"Probably just the wind," TJ said. She threw an angry scowl at Herby and Tuna, who floated above her desk examining the camera.

But instead of taking the hint, Herby called out, "Hey, Your Dude-ness, this is pretty torked."

"WHAT'S THAT?" Elizabeth cried, staring at her floating camera. "WHO SAID THAT?" If she was pale before, she was downright white now.

"You better check this out," Herby said.

Before TJ could make up any more excuses (like maybe Elizabeth was hallucinating and losing her mind), Herby opened another blade on his knife and

ting-tang-walla-walla bing

BANG!

the image in the camera's viewfinder came to life, smack-dab in the middle of TJ's bedroom—complete in all of its three-dimensional, holographic glory.

"AHHH!" Elizabeth screamed the type of scream most screamers scream when they see life-size copies of themselves standing in front of themselves. The only problem was, this life-size copy wasn't exactly standing.

"Turn it off!" Elizabeth cried. "How'd you do that?? TURN IT OFF!"

TJ tried to answer, but it's hard answering when you're busting a gut laughing. The reason was simple. Elizabeth had videotaped herself practicing dance moves . . . either that or somebody had plugged her into a 220-volt outlet and was electrocuting her—it was hard to tell by the way she kept jerking, writhing, and wrenching.

"Turn it off!" Elizabeth screamed. Unfortunately her screams were the type that could bring concerned fathers (and nosy sisters) into bedrooms, so Herby reached for the knife, pointed it at Elizabeth, and

Sizzle . . . sizzle

POP!

"   !" Elizabeth shouted. Then, grabbing her mouth, she tried again.
"   !!"

"Don't worry," TJ explained. "It's just the Volume Control. They used it on me, too. It's set on maximum intensity until you quiet down."

"   !!!" Elizabeth screamed.

"Actually, that's not quieting down."

"   !!!!!!"

"No, that's not it either."

Meanwhile, Tuna had found another scene in the camera. "This one's rather enlightening." He nodded to Herby, who pressed the first blade and

†ing-tang-Walla-walla bing

BANG!

the 3D image in front of them completely changed.

Well, not completely . . .

It was still Elizabeth, only now her face was up real close to the camera as she practiced her kissing technique. With lips pressed to the lens, she was making all kinds of smooching and smacking noises. And if that wasn't embarrassing enough, she began whispering: *"Yes, I know I'm gorgeous, so kiss me, you fool . . . kiss me . . . kiss me. . . ."*

"   !!!!!!!!!!" Elizabeth screamed. Her face had gone from pale white to traffic-light red.

"   !!!!!!!!!!!!!!!!!!!!"

"She's really not getting the hang of 'quieting down,' is she?" TJ asked.

Tuna looked at her sadly. "I'm afraid not."

"Uh-oh," Herby said as he looked at the viewfinder.

TJ turned to him. "Uh-oh, what?"

"This could be major quod-quod."

Tuna looked over Herby's shoulder and nodded. "I agree." He glanced to TJ and said, "They could very well burn you at the stake for this one."

"Burn who?" TJ asked. "Me?"

"Yes. Isn't that what your society does to witches?"

"Not anymore," TJ said. "Actually, witches are our heroes."

Tuna looked at her blankly. "Pardon me?"

"Oh yeah. They're in all our books and movies now. Witches, boy wizards, vampires—these days they're role models for all us kids."

"How zworked is that?" Herby said.

TJ was about to argue, then stopped, realizing he might have a point. She motioned to the camera. "So what is it? What do you see?"

Herby pressed the blade and another image appeared in the middle of the room—some pale-looking vampire dude (who needed a good hair brushing) fighting off werewolves over some girl who wanted to be just like him.

"What is it?" Tuna asked.

"Oh, that." TJ giggled. "That's just an old DVD she hasn't returned."

Herby tried again.

ting-tang-Walla-walla bing

BANG!

Suddenly, in the middle of the room sat a fire hydrant (about the same color as Elizabeth's traffic-light face). And it was talking! The valve where the hose attaches was moving like a pair of lips, and it was saying, *"Their names are Herby and Thomas Uriah Norman Alphonso the Third. They've come to take over the world."*

"It's Bruce Bruiseabone," Herby groaned.

"Take over the world?" Elizabeth's recorded voice asked from offscreen.

"That's right," the fire hydrant answered. *"And worse than that, they want to convince everyone that recycling is a bad idea."*

Elizabeth's offscreen voice grew excited. *"That's*

incredible! How are they going to do it? Take over the world, I mean."

"They've hidden their time pod in Thelma Jean Finkelstein's attic."

"You mean, CT's?"

"Close enough. They say they've run out of fuel, but it's really just a way to trick her into joining their evil plan."

"To take over the world?" Elizabeth repeated.

"And convince everyone that recycling is a bad idea."

Herby pressed Pause and the fire hydrant froze.

Tuna cleared his throat. "Well, that's certainly immature of Bruce, isn't it?"

"And risky," Herby chimed in, "with all the dogs in the neighborhood."

TJ stared at the image of the fire hydrant and frowned hard. Then she stared at the boys and frowned even harder.

Tuna fidgeted. "Surely you do not believe what he said about us."

Herby added, "We're big fans of recycling."

"And taking over the world?" TJ asked.

"What? No, absolutely not." Tuna shook his head. "He was simply spreading rumors."

"And we all know how wrong spreading rumors is," Herby said.

"Especially if they're about us," Tuna added.

TJ continued staring at the boys. To be honest, she wasn't sure what to think. Why, after all this time, were they still unable to fix their time-travel pod? Was it really broken or just an excuse to hang around and torment her? And what about their gizmos that always backfired . . . usually on her? Whom should she really trust—a talking fire hydrant . . . or the two goofballs floating above her desk—one with a shorting-out Swiss Army Knife, the other still wet from swimming with her pet goldfish?

She gave a deep, weary sigh. They never had to make decisions like this back in Missouri.

She turned to Elizabeth, hoping maybe she had an opinion. Unfortunately, Elizabeth had graduated from someone screaming silently in the middle of the room to someone huddled in the corner, whimpering and quivering like a bowl of Jell-O.

In some ways, TJ wished she could join her.

CHAPTER FOUR

Lunch with the Losers

TIME TRAVEL LOG:
Malibu, California, November 3

Begin Transmission
Shared my genius idea with subject. Even Tuna was impressed—well, until the part where everything went to quod-quod.

End Transmission

TJ was eating lunch at the Losers' Table with two of her four friends. The other two, ~~Gertrude~~ George and the hamster, were at home.

That left Naomi Simpletwirp, a tall, gangly AV geek who was always

Click-ing, clack-ing,

and

Crunch-ing

breath mints. At the moment she was popping them in between bites of her peanut butter sandwich (since no one likes peanut butter breath, and you can never be too careful).

Second, there was Naomi's kind-of boyfriend, who was also kind of a genius. Unfortunately, he not only had the world's worst hay fever, but he had the gold medal for the greatest number of times per minute you can wipe your nose on the back of your hand. (Actually, it's a pretty impressive award, though the medal is sorta slimy.)

His name? Doug

Sniff-snort

Claudlooper.

Naomi and Doug were both cool in their own wear-a-pocket-protector-and-tape-up-your-broken-glasses way. And together, the two could put on quite a

Click Sniff-sniff

clack snort-Snort

CRUNCH!

concert.

Across the cafeteria, Elizabeth Mindlessfan sat at Hesper Breakahart's table with all the other Hesper wannabes . . . and, of course, dreamy Chad. But it was hard for TJ to look at dreamy Chad when Elizabeth was sitting next to him and giving her the ever-popular stink-eye.

Still, TJ had little to fear. Last night the boys had erased Elizabeth's video and zapped her home with their Transporter Beam (after accidental side trips to Jupiter, the top of the Eiffel Tower, and a pigpen in Indiana). Eventually, she wound up asleep in her bed, thinking it was all a dream—well, almost. There were those five dozen flies that hitchhiked from Indiana and the fact that she could use a good bath.

But now, things were finally returning to normal. Unfortunately, that would be TJ's kind of normal.

"Did you see that my name is on Hesper's

click, clack

CRUNCH!

callback list?" Naomi asked in excitement.

"List?" TJ asked.

"Yeah (*sniff-snort*)," Doug said. "Callbacks to be on Hesper's TV show. They only asked five or six kids, and Naomi was one of them." He grinned at Naomi. "She's so **(SNIFF)**—"wow, that was a good one—"excited."

Luckily, everyone else was also excited. It seemed everybody was talking about who was and who was not on the callback list. In fact, it was such a hot topic that they almost forgot about TJ and the disappearing elephant.

Almost.

"And you're on it too," Naomi said, digging into

her backpack to find her toothbrush and toothpaste. (Naomi also has a thing about oral hygiene.)

"Me?" TJ asked in surprise.

"Sure. That stunt where you ran down the aisle with the elephant. I could tell that the

bruSh, bruSh

gargle, gargle
(Yep, she had mouthwash, too)

director was really impressed."

"Oh, that," TJ said. She tried to sound interested but was too busy checking the room for 23rd-century time travelers. Even though she'd given them strict orders to stay at home, she knew they'd sneak out in one of their morphed disguises to spy on her. They always did.

For example, take the Swiss cheese in her sandwich. Any one of those little holes could be their eyes peering out at her . . . which explains why she wadded up the sandwich and threw it into her bag.

"TJ?" Naomi asked in surprise.

"Guess I'm not hungry," TJ said.

And that two-sided napkin dispenser could easily be two faces, until

POW!

TJ swept it to the floor.

"TJ?" Doug sniffed.

"Sorry," she said. "Guess I'm a little clumsy today."

"It's just nerves," Naomi said. "We're all pretty excited for the chance to be on the TV show."

"Yeah," TJ muttered, eyeing the milk dispenser across the room with its two handles, one for 2%, the other for nonfat . . . or one for Herby's head and the other for Tuna's.

"You don't sound very excited," Naomi said, digging out her mint-flavored dental floss and going to work on her teeth.

"Why should I be?" TJ asked. She turned away from the milk dispenser in case the boys could read her lips. "Hesper can be such a jerk sometimes."

Naomi looked confused. "Sometimes?"

"Well, all right, *all* the time."

"But a famous jerk," Naomi argued.

"Actually, I think you two may be a little (*sniff-snort*) hard on Hesper," Doug said.

"What do you mean?" Naomi asked as she began digging for her breath spray.

"Maybe we shouldn't always be bad-mouthing her."

TJ eyed him suspiciously. He sounded strangely like Tuna from last night. Maybe the time traveler had disguised himself as Doug.

"What's wrong?" Doug asked.

TJ shook her head. No, not even goofy time travelers would want to be Doug Claudlooper.

"What's (*click-clack*) up?" Naomi said. She'd given up on the breath spray and gone back to the mints.

TJ shrugged. "It just seems like everyone's lecturing me on not saying bad stuff about people."

Doug started to answer, but he was interrupted by

WhOooo . . .

whaaaa . . .

Eeeeeee . . .

It was a strange sound, but not as strange as where it came from.

The clock above the cafeteria door. More precisely, the minute hand on the clock that was spinning backward and the hour hand that was spinning the opposite direction.

Then there was the screaming:

"Herby, what are you doing?!"

"I don't

WhOooo . . .

whaaaa . . .

Eeeeeee . . .

know. But somebody better stop this ride before I hurl!"

"Use the Time Freezer Blade!"

"Good

WhOooo . . .

whaaaa . . .

Eeeeeee . . .

thinking."

zzoo . . . o . . . o . . . . a . . . . . a .
. . . . a . . . . h . . . . h . . . .
. . . . .

With yet another strange sound, everyone
in the room started moving verrry verrrrrrry
sloooooooooowly. . . .

Everyone but TJ and

Krinkle . . . krackle

POOF!

Tuna and Herby.

The boys had morphed themselves into normal,
everyday people—normal, everyday people wearing
silver time-travel suits and floating above TJ's table.

"Guys!" she complained.

"Sorry, Your Dude-ness," Herby said. "The knife is
still fritzing out."

"I'm not talking about the knife!" She glanced
around the room. By now everyone was moving
slower than a kid heading home with a bad report
card.

Naomi was

cliiiiiiiiiiiiiiickkkkk,
claaaaaaaaaaaaaaaackkk

CRUUUUUUUUUUUUUUUNCH-ing

Doug was

sniiiiiiiiiiiiiiiiiiiiiiiiiiiiiifffff,
sniiiiiiiiiiiiiiiiiiiiiiiiiiiiifffff

snoooooooooooooooort-ing

And Elizabeth was still

glaaaaaaaaaaaaaaaaaaa
aaaaaaaaaaring

"I'm talking about you spying on me!" TJ
complained.

"Actually," Tuna said, "a more accurate word
would be *observing*."

"Yeah," Herby agreed, "definitely observing. Besides, it was Tuna's idea."

Tuna turned to him. "It most certainly was not."

"Yeah, dude, it was."

"It was not."

"Was too."

"Guys."

"Was not."

"Was too."

"Was—"

"GUYS!"

That did the trick. They finally stopped and faced her—well, after one more "Was not."

And one more "Was too."

"I don't care whose idea it was," TJ said. "We agreed you wouldn't follow me to school."

Herby frowned. "But how else can we spy on you?"

TJ gave him a look.

"After carefully studying our calculations," Tuna said, "I think we have a solution to your problem."

"You've fixed the time pod and are heading home?" TJ asked.

"Uh, no. But we've found a way to prove we're the ones telling the truth and not Bruce Bruiseabone."

"Oh," TJ said, trying to hide her disappointment.

Herby chimed in. "It's my best thought in days."

"Actually it's been your only thought," Tuna sighed.

"That's what I said."

"What is it?" TJ asked.

Herby proudly produced the Acme Thought Broadcaster Pen.

"Oh no," TJ groaned. "Not again."

Tuna explained, "We've changed frequencies so our thoughts will broadcast through cell phones. We just point the pen at ourselves and it will allow you to hear what we're really thinking through your speakerphone."

"That way you'll know we're telling the truth," Herby said.

TJ thought for a moment, then nodded slowly. "All right. That makes sense . . . as much as anything else you guys do."

"My thought exactly," Herby said. Without a further word, he pointed the pen at Tuna and clicked the top. A blue beam shot out the bottom, followed by the usual weird sound

Zibwaaa . . . Zibwaaa . . . zibwaaa

effects.

The good news was the beam worked perfectly. It struck Tuna and his thoughts were instantly broadcast through TJ's cell phone.

"See," he thought, *"it's working perfectly."*

And since Tuna's travel suit was silver, the beam reflected off the suit and also struck Herby.

Herby grinned and thought, *"Just like we planned."*

Unfortunately, the suit was so crumpled and crinkly that the beam not only bounced off Tuna and hit Herby . . . it bounced off Tuna and hit everybody! The thoughts of everyone in the school cafeteria started being broadcast through everyone's cell phones.

So when the beam hit the computer geeks' table, TJ could hear them thinking, *"Maaaccccccccs . . . . ruuuuuuuuuuule!"*

As it hit Hesper's wannabes' table, she could hear them thinking,

"IIIIIIIII . . . hooooooooope . . . nooooooo . . . ooooone . . . seeeeeeeees . . . myyyyyyyyyyyyyy . . . broooooooooookeeeeeeen . . . naaaaaaaaaaaail . . ."

And over at the jocks' table, she could hear them thinking,

TJ frowned, trying to hear what was going on in their heads . . . until she realized it was the jocks' table, which meant nothing was going on. Except for several

Scraaaaaaaatches

and a whole lot of

Buuuuuuuuuuuuuuurps

"*Turn it off!*" Tuna thought. "*Turn off the beam!*"
"*Relax,*" Herby thought as he reached for the Thought Broadcaster Pen. "*Don't get all gur-roid about it.*" He gave the pen a click and
"*PPPPPPPCCCCCCCCs . . . arrrrrrrrrrre . . . waaaaaaay . . . beeetteeeeerrrrrrrr!*"
"*I'IIIIIII . . . geeeeeeet . . . faaaaaaaaaat . . . eaaaaaaaaatiiiiing . . . thiiiiiiiiiiissss . . . whoooooooole*

*. . . stiiiiiiiiiiiiiiiick . . . offffffff . . .
ceeeeeellllllerrrrrrry!"*

And of course,

"What's wrong?" TJ thought. *"It's not working."*
"The pen is stuck!"
"Well, unstick it," she thought.
"Good thinking," Tuna thought back, then reached
into his pocket and pulled out the Swiss Army Knife.
He whipped open a blade and began digging around
the pen's clicker, trying to unstick it.

The only problem was that all his digging sort of

*Z . . . . Z . . . . o . . . . . .
o . . . . . o . . . o . . . a . . . a . . hhh*

reversed the Time Freezer Blade.

Suddenly everybody was moving and thinking at
regular speed. Which meant everyone was able to
hear everyone else's real thoughts at regular speed.
Which meant things were going to get real ugly
real fast.

OOPS!

"What have you done!" Tuna thought.
"What's going on?" TJ demanded.
Herby replied, *"We may be in for a little quod-quod."*

CHAPTER FIVE

Sharing a Thought

(actually, 327 of them)

TIME TRAVEL LOG:

Malibu, California, November 3—supplemental

Begin Transmission

Progress with subject is slow. Thought Broadcaster
Pen on fritz . . . again. Not helped by addition of
flying goat cheese (yuck!), Hostess Twinkies (yum!),
and computer geeks (look out!).

End Transmission

Everybody's cell phone broadcasting everybody
else's thoughts might have been okay if everybody
had been thinking halfway nice thoughts (or even

one-eighth-way nice thoughts). Unfortunately, that wasn't the case. Take, for instance, the action happening over at the computer geeks' table:

Computer Geek #1 leaped to his feet. "You think your iPhone is superior to my Droid!"

"I didn't say that," Computer Geek #2 replied, then thought, *"However, if you weren't such a moron, the fact would be obvious."*

Then there was the jock table:

Okay, still not much happening there. But there was definitely action at Hesper's table.

"What?" Hesper leaped to her feet and shouted at Chad. "You don't think I'm the prettiest and most adorable girl in school?!"

"I didn't say that," Chad replied, then thought, *"But you sure are the loudest."*

"I heard that, mister!"

And Trent Tauntalot, who sat one table over,

didn't help much by thinking, *"You should ask him how he feels about the New Kid."*

Chad looked at Trent in disbelief.

While Hesper glared at Chad in disbelief. "What does he mean?"

Chad shook his head, deciding not to talk. Unfortunately his mind decided to think, *"Trent's a jerk. Don't listen to him."* Glancing toward TJ's table, he continued, *"But she is kinda cute . . . I mean, for someone who has mental issues."*

Hesper spun around to glare at TJ. (It's best I don't repeat what she thought. But if looks could kill, someone should be calling 911.)

Finally, there were TJ's thoughts. *"He likes me? Did he say he likes me? I can't believe he likes me! Dreamy Chad Steel with those dreamy blue eyes actually likes— STOP IT! EVERYONE CAN HEAR WHAT YOU'RE THINKING!"* She almost managed to stop, until her eyes drifted to Chad's. *"'Mrs. TJ Steel,' I like the sound of that. STOP IT! I wonder if our children will have those same dreamy blue—STOP IT! STOP IT! STOP IT!"*

Talk about dying of embarrassment. Forget 911. Call the nearest funeral home for pickup and delivery.

Even with that, things could have been okay (well, not okay, but a lot less messy), except for—

WARNING TO READER: If you are a neat freak or have food allergies, please be advised to skip this portion and proceed directly to page 75.

Since Computer Geek #1 did not appreciate Computer Geek #2's earlier thought (let alone the ones you missed about his acne, his ugly sister, and his parents' *used* car—remember, this is Malibu), Computer Geek #1 picked up his cup of brown rice topped with tasteless tofu (who eats this stuff, anyway?) and

DUMP-ed

it all over the head of his new ex-best-friend.

Not to be outdone, Geek #2 took his organically grown sprouts and goat cheese sandwich (which tastes even worse than tofu) and

SMEAR-ed

it across the shirt of *his* new ex-best-friend.

Meanwhile, the jocks, who still did not have a thought but knew an excuse for a good food fight

when they saw one, joined in. This would explain
the flying protein shakes, the sailing pizzas, and
tossed chairs. (Sometimes jocks get carried away.)

Meanwhile, Hesper scrunched her perfectly
plucked brows into a frown so that her perfectly
zit-free forehead almost showed a wrinkle. This
meant all the other Hesper wannabes scrunched
their perfectly plucked brows, almost wrinkling their
perfectly zit-free foreheads, until they were

SMACK-ed,

SMASH-ed,

and

SpLUNK-ed

by flying pizzas, goat cheese sandwiches . . . and the
ever-popular Hostess Twinkie or two. (Some kids are
lucky enough to pack their own lunches.)

Soon everybody in the cafeteria, all 327 of them,
was in a major food fight. You name it, it was being
hurled.

Bananas were

FLING, FLING, FLING-ing

Granola bars were

ZING, ZING, ZING-ing

Celery was

(well, celery doesn't have quite the same oomph or splat factor as other foods, but it was the best Hesper's calorie-starved group could offer)

And thanks to the jocks, besides chairs, entire lunch tables were now

"LOOK OUT! INCOMING!"

"HERBY!" TJ shouted. "TUNA! DO SOMETHING!"

"NO PROBLEM, YOUR DUDE-NESS," Herby shouted. "I'VE GOT IT UNDER CONTROL!" Unfortunately, this was followed by what he was really thinking, which was something like, *"Oh, boy, we're really zworked."*

But somehow, against all odds, Herby did something right. Well, almost. Eventually, TJ heard

Chugga-Chugga-Chugga

BLING!

And just like that, the Transporter Blade transported her out of the cafeteria and landed her, safe and sound, in

ROAR!

the middle of a zoo's polar bear exhibit.
"HERBY!"
"NO PROB, YOUR BABE-NESS, I'M ON IT."

Chugga-Chugga-Chugga

BLING!

And just like that, she landed, safe and sound, on

ROAr!

the runway of a busy airport (complete with a 747 coming in for a landing right on top of her)!
"HERBY!"
"HANG ON!"

Chugga-Chugga-Chugga

BLING!

Finally, at long last, TJ landed safe and sound, standing in

slosh, slosh,

"Ewww!"

the toilet bowl of her

"I'll never wear these shoes again!"

bathroom.

* * * * *

Back at school, things eventually settled down— as soon as people ran out of food to toss and the jocks ran out chairs, tables, and computer geeks. (Sometimes they *really* get carried away.)

Needless to say, it was all pretty weird and everyone had lots to think about (except the jocks).

Chad was grateful Hesper's limo had picked her up early from school for an interview she had on *MTV* (*M*indless *T*elevision *V*iewing network). He hoped the walk home by himself would give him time to clear his head. But thanks to cell phones and Hesper's motormouth, it didn't happen. Come to think of it, it never happened.

"So it was all just a joke, right?" she asked over his phone. "You really don't have a thing for the New Kid, right? I mean, you still think I'm way cuter, right? And more adorable, right? And more beautiful and funnier and . . ."

It's not that Hesper Breakahart was self-centered or anything. She just knew there was

> —no one on the planet more interesting than herself
> —no one more interesting to talk about than herself
> —no one more qualified to talk about herself than herself

So Chad never got a word in edgewise, topwise, bottomwise, or anywise. And though he tried to pay attention, her voice always wound up sounding like

"Blah, blah, blah

blah, blah, blah"

Since his participation really wasn't necessary, he slipped the phone into his pocket, which reduced her volume to

"Blah, blah, blah

blah, blah, blah"

so she could continue talking and he could continue thinking. Not a bad plan, until:
"Hey, Chad,

CLICK, CLACK

SNIFF-SNORT!

wait up!"

He turned to see Naomi Simpletwirp and Doug Claudlooper running toward him. Although they weren't on Malibu Junior High's A-list of popular students (come to think of it, they hadn't even made the Z-list), Chad enjoyed their company. Like the New Kid, there was something real and down-to-earth about them—despite Doug's perpetual *sniff-sniff*-ing and Naomi's *click, clack*-ing.

"Boy, what a day," Doug said as they arrived.

"Yeah," Chad agreed.

"Everyone's talking about what you thought about TJ," Naomi said as she dug into her pocket for a breath strip.

"Who?"

"TJ, the New Kid."

"Oh, her." Chad shook his head. "I don't know what I was thinking."

"Well, (*sniff-sniff*) everybody else does," Doug said.

"Yeah. What do you suppose caused that," Chad asked, "where everybody was hearing everybody's thoughts?"

Doug shrugged. "We're still running tests." Besides holding records in back-of-the-hand nose-wiping, Doug was a world-class scientist.

"So, is it true?" Naomi asked.

"Is what true?

"That you like TJ?"

"Like her?" Chad scoffed. "No way. Forget it. I don't know what you're talking about. That's crazy."

"You're sure working hard at saying no," Doug said.

"What's that supposed to mean?"

Naomi answered, "It means, who are you trying to convince . . . us or yourself?"

"Look, she's a nice kid and I feel sorry for her, being new and everything. And then there's her whole speech problem."

"Speech problem?" Doug asked.

"You know, where she can barely talk," Chad said.

"Actually—" Naomi popped another breath mint in her mouth—"that's just around you. She talks fine till she gets around you."

Chad frowned. "You've said that before, but I still don't get why."

Naomi looked at him. "You're kidding me, right?"

Chad looked at her, waiting for an explanation.

She turned to Doug.

Doug looked at her, waiting for an explanation.

Naomi rolled her eyes. "Guys . . . you really are clueless about girls, aren't you?"

Chad blinked.

Doug blinked.

"Oh, brother." Naomi was just about to work in another good eye roll when they were interrupted by

"LOOK OUT, LOSERS!"

They spun around and barely leaped off the sidewalk in time as Trent Tauntalot skateboarded between them with his mandatory bad-guy cackle and a little taunt thrown in for Chad. "Nice move in the cafeteria today, Romeo! You startin' a harem with all them girlfriends?"

Of course, Chad responded with the ever-brilliant "Hey!" (always a great comeback) until something more intelligent came to mind. "I'm seeing Hesper, all right? And she's the most beautiful and clever and witty and fantastic girl in the whole world!"

"And if you don't believe him," Doug shouted, "you can ask her!"

Chad gave Doug a look, and Doug gave Chad a shrug.

And not to be ignored, Hesper Breakahart continued her

"Blah, blah, blah

blah, blah, blah"-ing

CHAPTER SIX

Birdbrain Solutions

TIME TRAVEL LOG:

Malibu, California, November 4

Begin Transmission

*Here, kitty, kitty, kitty—er, KITTY, **KITTY, KITTY . . .**"*

End Transmission

Later that evening, while TJ was bruising her brain over complex fractions, there was a knock on her door.

"TJ?" It was Dad.

She threw a glance around the room. She'd banished the guys upstairs to the attic but wanted to

make sure they hadn't sneaked down to spy on her
. . . or take laps around the fishbowl. Sometimes a
person just needs her own space.

When she was sure it was safe, she called, "Come
on in, Daddy."

He opened the door and entered. He looked
really tired. "Your sister said you were having a
couple rough days."

TJ snorted. "Since when does Violet think about
anything but Violet."

"TJ."

"Well, except for what other people think about
Violet."

He gave her a look.

She shrugged. "Sorry."

Dad crossed to where she sat at the desk. "She
says you and that movie star—Heather, Harriet,
Henri—"

"Hesper," TJ said. "Hesper Breakahart."

"She says you and Hesper aren't getting along so
well."

"Somebody should knock that princess off her
throne."

"TJ . . ."

It was a rotten thing to say, but rotten was exactly
how she felt. "Sorry."

She was glad Dad decided not to go into one of his world-famous lectures. Instead, he reached into his pocket and pulled out a necklace with a thin gold chain and a pinkish-white stone.

TJ stared. "Is that . . . Mom's?"

"Yeah, her opal necklace." His voice grew husky. "I was going through her jewelry box tonight and found it. Opal—that was her birthstone, right?"

TJ nodded. She could feel her eyes begin to burn as she watched him carefully unfasten the latch.

He cleared his throat. "It looks pretty silly on me, so I figured . . . I figured maybe you'd like it."

"Me?" Her own voice grew husky.

Dad said nothing more as he bent over to gently place it around her neck.

Tears filled TJ's eyes and her throat grew so tight she could barely talk. "Oh, Daddy . . ."

"It was one of her—" he coughed slightly—"one of her favorites."

Before she could stop them, tears spilled onto her cheeks. She tried wiping them away, but more just kept coming.

He forced a chuckle. "Hey, this is supposed to cheer you up, not make you sad."

She tried to answer but could only nod.

It took forever for his thick fingers to fasten the

clasp. "You know, in all the years we were married, I never heard your mother say anything bad about someone."

TJ glanced down and watched as a tear splattered onto the page of her math book.

"To be honest, I don't know how she did it. I asked her once, and do you know what she said?"

TJ shook her head.

"She said the key isn't what you say—it's what you think. Whenever somebody got on her nerves, she tried to think something nice about them." At last he fastened the chain. "There we go."

She shifted in her seat to look at him, but he glanced away, his own eyes shiny with moisture. "You know, you're a lot like her . . . your mother." He swallowed and continued. "And I bet somehow, you'll be able to do the same. Think good thoughts, I mean."

TJ could barely see him through her tears.

"Well—" he took a deep breath—"I've wasted enough of your time." He bent down, kissed the top of her head, and stepped toward the door.

"Daddy?" she croaked.

He stopped but did not turn.

"Thank you."

He nodded. It was obvious he didn't want her to

see his tears. "Good night" was all he said. Then he strode into the hallway and quietly shut her door.

TJ reached up and ran her fingers over the opal. *"Whenever somebody got on her nerves, she tried to think something nice about them."* Her cell phone rang and she pulled it from her pocket. When she answered, her voice was still thick with emotion. "Hello?"

"JT? This is Hesper Breakahart. I just want to tell you the good news."

TJ wiped her face. "Good news?"

"Uh-huh. Oh, this is sooo exciting. The producers and I have reached our decision."

"Decision?"

"About my TV show, silly."

TJ frowned, trying to remember.

"Anyway, we had a long talk, and since my little sister is supposed to wear stupid glasses, and since you already wear them, we decided *YOU* get to play the part. Isn't that fantastic?"

TJ's mind raced trying to catch up.

"We film the day after tomorrow and I wanted to be the first to call up and congratulate you. So . . . congratulations."

Somewhere in the back of her mind, TJ remembered her manners and muttered a quiet "Thank . . . you."

"Oh, you're welcome, TB. We're going to have such super fun. Well, tootles." And just like that, Hesper hung up.

TJ sat for another long moment. Super fun? With Hesper Breakahart? Darker thoughts quickly surfaced. What was the girl *really* up to? Then, scolding herself, TJ reached up to her mother's necklace. She had to think of something positive. Anything. Anything at all.

She had it:

Hesper had hung up, so TJ didn't have to talk to her anymore—at least for tonight.

Okay, it wasn't much, but it was a start. Unfortunately, Thelma Jean Finkelstein would need a lot more than a start to survive Hesper Breakahart's newest plan.

* * * * *

Of course, TJ broke the news to her family. But before she could tell them that she had doubts about doing the show, Dad was on the phone bragging to Aunt Matilda and all the relatives back home. (TJ still thought of Missouri as home.) Then there was her sister Violet, who was already on the computer starting a TJ Finkelstein Fan Club, creating a special page on Facelook, and selling locks of TJ's hair on eekBay. And little sister Dorie? For whatever reason, Dorie thought TJ was already a star no matter what she did. (Kids—go figure.) In any case, TJ soon realized there was really no way out. She would have to do the show.

The next morning, as she walked Dorie to the bus stop, she started making plans.

1. She'd apologize to Chad Steel for any misunderstanding. No problem. All she had to do was learn how to talk in front of him.

2. She vowed to herself never, *ever* to use (or even think) the word *dreamy*.

3. . . . Well, there would have been a third if she hadn't been interrupted by two 23rd-century boys floating beside her.

"Guys," she whispered, then stole a look at Dorie. Luckily, Dorie was listening to her iPod and rocking out to Bert and Ernie, or Kermit, or (gulp) Barney. "Guys!"

Tuna looked at her in surprise. "Oh, hello there. Fancy meeting you here."

"I said you could *not* follow me to school."

"Follow you?" Herby asked from her other side. "We're not following you."

"Of course not," Tuna said. "To follow you we would have to be behind you, and as you can clearly see, we are beside you. Therefore, technically we are not—"

"GUYS!"

TJ's shout startled Dorie. The little girl hit Pause and looked around. "Are you talking to the ghosts again?" she whispered.

"Ghosts!" Herby yelled.

"Where?!" Tuna cried.

TJ coughed, trying to cover their voices. "Now, Dorie, you know there are no such things as ghosts."

"Whew," Herby sighed.

"That's a relief," Tuna agreed.

TJ continued louder. "Ghosts are just make-believe. You know that."

"Right." Dorie glanced around nervously. "But do they?"

Herby leaned toward Tuna. "Do we?"

"Oh, look," TJ said, grateful to change subjects, "there's your bus."

The big yellow vehicle rounded the corner and pulled to a stop just up the street. Before Dorie could react, TJ hugged her, turned her toward the bus, and gave her a push. The child skipped toward it as happy as a clam.

"Kids," Tuna sighed. "So cute—"

"And trusting," Herby added.

"And clueless," TJ said, smiling and waving to Dorie as she stepped onto the bus.

With a belch of black smoke, it pulled from the curb and headed down the street. Once it was out of sight, TJ put her hands on her hips and glared.

"So." Tuna nervously cleared his throat. "You will be happy to know we have found a solution to your problem."

"Which one?" TJ said.

"Which one?" he repeated.

TJ nodded. "Since you two decided to help me, I've got more than I can count."

"Actually, Your Dude-ness," Herby said, "Tuna would be the one to blame for that."

"Me?" Tuna said. "I most certainly am not."

"You most certainly are."

"Guys."

"Am not."

"Are too."

"GUYS!"

"Not."

"Too."

"Not."

"I know you are but what am I."

Herby's phrase stopped Tuna cold. Both TJ and Tuna stared at him.

"Sorry." He shrugged. "I just wanted to fit that in."

"Nevertheless," Tuna said, "we have corrected the malfunction in the Acme Thought Broadcaster Pen."

"Sold at 23rd-century time-travel stores everywhere," Herby added.

"It will now penetrate our time-travel suits and broadcast our true thoughts and intentions." Tuna reached into his pocket and handed her the pen.

TJ frowned. "Why do I need to know your thoughts again?"

"To decide who is to be trusted—Bruce Bruiseabone or your longtime friends of . . ." He turned to Herby. "How long have we been her longtime friends?"

Herby glanced at his right shoelace and read the time. "For 24 days, 12 hours, 19 minutes, and 31 seconds."

TJ nodded. Somehow it seemed longer.

Still staring at his shoelace, Herby read, "Make that 24 days, 12 hours, 19 minutes, and *33* seconds."

Reluctantly she took the pen Tuna had been holding out to her. It didn't look any different than when it was broken.

"Wait—24 days, 12 hours, 19 minutes, and *38* seconds."

"Just point it at us, press the clicker on the top, and fire," Tuna said.

"24 days, 12 hours, 19 minutes, and *42* seconds."

Tuna threw an irritated look to his partner. "The sooner the better."

Herby nodded and added, "24 days, 12 hours, 19 minutes, and *49* seconds."

TJ glanced around to make sure no one was watching. Then she aimed the pen at Herby, fired it, and

Zibwaaa . . . zibwaaa . . . zibwaaa

POOF!

Tuna cringed at the last sound and turned to Herby. "You told me you fixed it!"

"I did," Herby thought.

The good news was the beam worked exactly like it was supposed to. They could hear Herby's thoughts perfectly. The bad news was . . . well, Tuna was about to find out.

"But," Tuna argued, "that last sound it made—it's just like the Morphing Blade." His face filled with fear.

"Don't tell me you fixed the Thought Broadcaster Pen with parts from the Morphing Blade!"

"All right."

"Did you?"

"I can't tell you," Herby thought.

"Why not?"

"You just told me not to."

Tuna began to pace. *"*I can't believe it! You can be so mindless, sometimes!"

"Hey, who you calling mindless?"

"You, you birdbrain!"

"Listen, dude, if anybody's a birdbrain around here, it's you!"

And just like that

POOF!

Tuna turned into a bird. Fortunately, he was not one of those boring birds with boring brown feathers. Instead, he was a beautiful yellow canary (not that he appreciated the difference).

He began flying around and angrily

Warble, warble, warble-ing

"What's he want?" TJ cried.

Herby motioned to the pen. *"Turn the beam on him and hear what he's thinking."*

TJ pointed the pen at Tuna, fired

Zibwaaa . . . zibwaaa . . . zibwaaa

POOF!

and now she could also hear Tuna's thoughts.

"Look what you've done!" he thought. *"Look what you've done!"*

"I guess that'll teach you to call me a birdbrain," Herby thought smugly.

"You are *a birdbrain!"* Tuna thought.

And just like that,

POOF!

Herby also became a bird. But instead of a canary (whose warbling was so bad it made your eyes water), Herby was a goofy-looking robin with long surfer feathers hanging in his eyes.

"Uh-oh," Herby thought. *"This isn't turning out so good."*

"You think?" Tuna thought, ruffling his feathers in anger.

But the fun and games weren't entirely over. Because suddenly there was a brand new player on the field. One who came in the form of a giant, two-story, talking

"well, hello again, blokes"

cat.

Now normally, two-story talking cats are not a problem (though I would hate to empty their litter box). But in this case there were two minor concerns:

Minor Concern #1:
All cats, regardless of their size (or fake English accents) eat birds.

Minor Concern #2:
Herby instantly recognized the cat to be . . .

"Bruce Bruiseabone! What do we do?"

Tuna had only one answer. *"FLY!!!"*

And fly they did . . . with Chatty Kitty bounding after them, right on their heels—er, tails . . . er, whatever birds have—which left TJ standing all alone in utter amazement and thinking, *This is definitely not one of my better days.*

Unfortunately, the day was still young.

CHAPTER SEVEN

Birdies and Bullies

TIME TRAVEL LOG:

Malibu, California, November 4–supplemental

Begin Transmission
Acme Thought Broadcaster Pen is fritzier than
ever. Thanks to someone's repair skills (and I'm not
naming names, especially if they're mine), it not
only broadcasts people's thoughts but it also turns
those thoughts into reality. We could be in some
outloopish quod-quod!

End Transmission

School was about to start and Chad was hanging out with his buddy Scott by the lockers. Like

everyone else, he was still weirded out about having his thoughts broadcast during yesterday's lunch. No one was sure how it happened, though rumor had it the computer geeks had played another practical joke. Granted, it wasn't very funny (computer geeks aren't famous for their sense of humor), but it was a lot better than last month's practical joke—the one where they programmed a guided missile to hit the school. Not the whole school, more like Coach Steroidson's gymnasium. (Besides having a lousy sense of humor, geeks aren't fond of PE.)

A moment later, Chad heard a voice. "Um, er, uh, *cough-cough*."

The New Kid was standing behind him—at least for the moment. With the way she was shaking and wobbling, he wasn't sure how long the standing part would last.

"Hey, you okay?" he asked.

"*Cough-cough*, uh, er, um," she answered.

She still had the speech problem, but he was proud of her for trying. He was also strangely happy. Odd, but whenever she was around him, it made him feel that way. Concerned that she might fall over, he took her arm. "Here, maybe you should lean against the lockers. You're sure you're okay?"

She nodded, though she might have been more

convincing if her eyes weren't glazed over and all dreamy-like.

"Congratulations, BLT."

They both turned to see Elizabeth Mindlessfan, Hesper's best friend since forever.

"I hear the producers picked you to be on Hesper's TV show."

Somehow the New Kid pried her eyes away from Chad and looked at Elizabeth. Her dreamy glaze shifted into cautious suspicion.

Elizabeth continued. "I just want you to know there are no hard feelings. I mean, even though I'd die to be on the show and I look way more like Hesper than you do—" she lowered her voice—"not to mention I come from the same planet—I just want you to know I couldn't be happier. So congratulations." She forced a dazzling, every-tooth-in-place smile (which could also pass for a sneering, every-fang-in-place snarl), then continued down the hall.

She'd barely left before Trent Tauntalot appeared. "Hey, check out the two lovebirds." Looking at the New Kid, he added, "So when you getting married and having all those Chad babies?"

Chad glanced at the New Kid. If she had trouble talking before, she was having trouble breathing now.

"Come on, man," Chad said. "Go easy on her."

"Why?" Trent spoke louder so everyone could hear. "'Cause she's *in love* with someone else's boyfriend?"

A handful of girls giggled.

"Come on," Chad said, "give her a break."

Trent stepped closer, getting into Chad's face. "And what're you gonna do if I don't?"

The New Kid turned and started to leave until Trent reached out his arm and blocked her. "Stick around, sweetie. Don't you want to see if your boyfriend has the guts to be a real man?"

Chad tried to pull Trent's arm away. "Okay, that's enough."

"And what if I say it isn't?" Trent pushed Chad away and grabbed the New Kid. Of course, Chad tried to help her, but Trent took advantage of his weight and shoved him hard against the lockers. "What do you think now, lover boy?" He held him tightly. "What do you think now?"

It was about this time that Chad noticed some very strange things:

First, the New Kid pulled out a very strange-looking pen and pointed it at him.

Second, the pen made a very strange

Zibwaaa . . . zibwaaa . . . zibwaaa

POOF!

sound.

Third, a very strange blue beam shot from the very strange pen and hit Chad directly in the face. It only lasted a moment, but just like yesterday, Chad's thoughts were broadcast through everybody's cell phones:

"I think you should stop pretending to be a tough guy and tell people what your real problem is."

And the fourth very strange thing was Trent *had* to do exactly what Chad thought! (But don't worry, since this book is rated G, we'll *bleep* out the bad stuff):

"Listen, you *bleep bleep bleep bleep, bleep bleep bleep bleep bleep bleep bleep bleep bleep bleep.* And furthermore, *bleep bleep bleep bleep bleep bleep bleep—*"

Well, that's not going to work. Okay, here's a quick summary of what Trent said:

"I just want to be liked. . . . Wait a minute. I can't believe people heard that! Well, I'll make sure they don't hear the part about Daddy thinking I'm a wimp just 'cause I cry when I watch all those chick flicks with Mommy, which is why I got to prove to him I'm a real man by making fun of everybody and fighting them no matter how scared I really am of them! Oh no, I can't believe they heard that, too! Now they know everything!! Well, except the part of wetting my bed. Oh no, why can't I stop saying this stuff?! I guess I'll just have to run home and have a good, long cry."

(Or something like that.)

* * * * *

By the time first period rolled around, everybody knew three very weird things:

VERY WEIRD THING #1: TJ had gotten the part on Hesper's TV show.
VERY WEIRD THING #2: Chad Steel had risked his life and limb standing up to a big ninth grader to protect TJ's honor.

VERY WEIRD THING #3: The big ninth grader had run home in tears (and might be watching a good chick flick with his mom).

Meanwhile in *PE* (previously established as *P*hysical *E*mbarrassment), Coach Steroidson was making everyone stand in front of a mirror and learn a little ballet. Not that TJ minded. She'd always dreamed of being the world's greatest ballerina. Unfortunately, those dreams interfered with her current title of World's Greatest Klutz. We're not talking *klutz* as in tripping over a rock or bumping into people. We're talking *klutz* as in tripping over painted crosswalks and falling over your shadow.

Anyway, Coach Steroidson had the CD cranked up to one notch below bust-your-eardrums as she shouted, "And down . . . and up. Plié . . . relevé . . . plié . . . relevé . . ."

They were easy ballet moves—just squatting down when she yelled, "Plié" and rising onto your toes when she yelled, "Relevé." Anybody could do it. Even TJ . . . if it wasn't for that klutz thing, which meant she was pliéing when the rest of the girls were relevéing, and relevéing when they were pliéing.

Although every girl in class was a perfect dancer (since every girl in Malibu starts dance class the day after she's born—the first day is spent getting manicures and visiting the tanning salon), Hesper Breakahart was still the best.

"Perfect!" Coach Steroidson shouted. "Hesper, you are so gifted."

TJ didn't want to complain, but she wondered if Hesper's "giftedness" had anything to do with the two stunt doubles she had beside her . . . one pliéing, the other relevéing.

"Oh, thank you so much," Hesper called as she stood sipping her sparkling water. "I guess it just comes naturally."

"You really are terrific," Elizabeth shouted to her.

"Why, thank you . . . uh, er . . ."

"Elizabeth," Elizabeth reminded her. "Your best friend since forever."

TJ glanced around the room, shaking her head in disbelief. Even Naomi was good—despite the compact mirror she was constantly checking herself out in.

"Psst, TJ?" Naomi whispered while pliéing.

"What?" TJ whispered back while relevéing.

"Does this T-shirt make me look fat?"

"Of course not," TJ said. "You look great."

"Great?" Naomi cried in alarm. "Is that all?! This is Malibu! I have to look perfect!"

And so they continued, up and down and up
and down (or in TJ's case, down and up and down
and up) until two birds flew from the girls' locker
room into the gymnasium. One just happened to
be a robin with a Swiss Army Knife in its talons.
The other was a yellow canary holding an Acme
Thought Broadcaster Pen in its little beak (obviously
stolen from TJ's locker). They circled high overhead
as everyone began shouting and pointing in excitement—everyone except TJ, who was groaning and
dropping her head in dismay.

"Your Dude-ness?" Herby thought.

"Great news!" Tuna added.

Of course their thoughts were clearly heard
through Coach Steroidson's CD player. And even
though TJ tried to wave them off, they landed on
her shoulders—the robin with the goofy bangs on her
right, the canary on her left.

"Guys," she whispered, "not now."

"But we've got way cool news!" the robin thought.

Everyone had stopped pliéing and relevéing. (It's
hard pliéing and relevéing when you're listening to
bird thoughts through a CD player.) Well, everyone
had stopped but TJ. She just kept going up when she
should be going down and going down when she
should be going up.

"The Time Freezer Blade," she whispered to them as she smiled helplessly at the class.

"What?" the canary thought while hopping about on her shoulder.

"The Time Freezer," she repeated. "Slow everyone down so they can't hear."

"Cool," the robin agreed. Immediately he tried opening the knife. But if you've ever been a bird with two little bird feet and a little bird beak, you know how hard it is to open a Swiss Army Knife.

"Uh, Your Dude-ness, a little help here?"

Still smiling at the class (and going up when she should be going down), TJ reached to her shoulder. She held the knife steady while the robin pecked at the blade a half-dozen times before it finally opened and

zZOo . . . o . . . o . . . . a . . . . . a . . . . . . a . . . . h . . . . h . . . .

CHAPTER EIGHT

From Bad to Baddester

TIME TRAVEL LOG:

Malibu, California, November 4–supplemental

Begin Transmission

Ever have one of those days? Our subject is having one of those lives.

End Transmission

As expected, everything in the gym turned to slow motion.

The music plaaaaaaaaaaaaaaaaaaaaaaaaaaaayed in slow motion.

Coach Steroidson shouuuuuuuuuuuuuuuuted in slow motion.

And everyone staaaaaaaaaaaaaaaaaared in slow motion.

Now the boys were thinking so fast no one but TJ could hear them.

"We need you to fire the Acme Thought Broadcaster Pen at us again," Tuna thought as he flitted about on her shoulder.

"So we can think ourselves back into humans and repair it," Herby thought from her other shoulder.

"Can't you just think it and it will happen?" TJ asked.

"The effects have worn off," Tuna explained.

"We need another blast, Your Dude-ness—as fast as you can."

"What's the rush?" TJ asked.

"As a canary, Tuna keeps wanting to sing."

"And that's a problem?"

"Picture sirens screaming, brakes squealing, and cats fighting . . . all at the same time."

"Is he that bad?" TJ asked.

"Worse," Herby thought.

TJ reached for the pen.

"Make certain you fire it for only a moment," Tuna warned.

"Because . . ."

"If the beam hits too long, the effects become irreversible."

"Meaning . . ."

"It would permanently give us power to change reality with our thoughts."

TJ shuddered. (The idea of Herby or Tuna having that type of power would make anyone shudder.) "Who should I fire this at first?" she asked.

"That would be me," Tuna thought.

"Why you, dude?"

"Because I was the one who conceived the plan."

"You did not."

"I most certainly did."

"Did not."

"Did too."

"Guys."

"Not."

"Too."

"Guys!" TJ finally stopped their bickering. Well, almost.

"If you don't fire the beam at me first, I will start singing," Tuna threatened.

"Okay, okay! Do him first!" Herby thought. *"Do him first!"*

TJ nodded. "Hop off my shoulder and onto the dance bar so I get a clear shot."

Tuna obeyed and fluttered over to the bar. Unfortunately, besides singing, canaries do a lot of flitting and hopping.

"Hold still," TJ ordered as she took aim.

"I'm trying," Tuna thought as he continued to flit and hop.

"Hurry, Your Dude-ness! Before he breaks into song!"

TJ took aim, held her breath, and

Zibwaaa . . . zibwaaa . . . zibwaaa

fired.

Unfortunately, she wasn't a great shot. Come to think of it, she wasn't even a good one. The beam completely missed Tuna and hit the mirror behind him.

Unfortunatelier, it bounced off the mirror and directly into Naomi's little makeup mirror.

Unfortunateliest, it bounced off Naomi's mirror and smack-dab into TJ's

POOf!

face.

And the unfortunateliest unfortunatelier (sorry about the grammar) was the beam seemed to paralyze TJ, so she just kept pointing the pen and it just kept on

POOF!

POOF!

POOF!

firing.

"Turn it off, Your Dude-ness! Turn it off!"

But TJ could not move.

In desperation, Tuna and Herby flew to her hand and started

jump-jump-jump-ing

on it and

peck-peck-peck-ing

it.

Nothing worked. Until, unable to stop himself, Tuna opened his beak and broke into the world's worst

Warble, Warble, warble-ing

The good news was the singing was so bad that TJ dropped the Acme Thought Broadcaster. And as it clattered to the ground, she regained consciousness.

The bad news was she was thinking, *"No offense, Tuna, but your voice sounds like fingernails on a blackboard."*

And why was that bad news, you ask?

(You are asking, right?)

Because it meant Tuna immediately went from some very bad warbling to some even worse

Screeeeetch-ing, scraaaaatch-ing,

and

scraaaaap-ing

"Uh-oh," TJ said.

"Uh-oh," Herby agreed.

"Did I do that?" TJ asked.

"You did that," Herby agreed.

Of course, Tuna would have loved to join the conversation, but he was too busy

Screeeeetch-ing, scraaaaatch-ing,

and

scraaaaap-ing

"That's going to last for a while, isn't it?" TJ said.

"Probably forever," Herby agreed.

"Oops," TJ said.

"Oops," Herby agreed.

* * * * *

Dinner with TJ's family that night was stranger than her regular, run-of-the-mill strange. In fact, on a scale of 1 to 10, we're talking a 12½. I won't bore you with the details, just the headlines:

LOCAL FAMILY EXCITED BY TV DEBUT

Well, everyone in the family was excited but TJ.
She had a few other things on her mind, like . . .

LOCAL HOUSE STALKED BY BIRDS

Tuna and Herby kept flying around the outside of the
house, begging her to let them inside and to change
them back. She would have, but she wanted to think
things through first. Which leads us to . . .

LOCAL GIRL BATTLES WEIRD THOUGHTS

Not only did TJ have to be careful what she said
about people, but thanks to the Acme Thought
Broadcaster Pen, she had to be careful what she
thought about them. And if you don't believe me,
just ask

    —the obnoxious barking dog across the street
who suddenly got laryngitis
    —Dorie's obnoxious, shedding cat who
suddenly went bald
    —the obnoxious Gossip Lady on TV who

suddenly told everyone *her own* secret problems—
like a loser boyfriend she was going to dump and
her lip implants and how bad her feet smelled

So you can see why TJ had to be extra careful
around the dinner table. Especially since it was her
night to cook and Violet always felt it was her duty
to point out what TJ did wrong.

"You know, TJ," she said, "you might have under-
cooked these green BBs just a bit.

"Those aren't BBs; they're peas," TJ said, while
thinking, *And I hope they make you come down with a
bad case of–NO, NO! I'M NOT GOING TO THINK
THAT! I'M NOT GOING TO THINK THAT!*

Little Dorie didn't help much when she piped in
with "But this yellow glue is sure yummy."

"That's macaroni and cheese," TJ said, while thinking, *You're cute, but sometimes I wish you'd just–NO,
NO, STOP IT!*

"Well, I think it's perfect," Dad said, crunching
away on the mashed potatoes.

"Sorry about your tooth," TJ said.

"Nonsense." He grinned, showing the gap where
he'd just broken a front tooth. "Sometimes mashed
potatoes can be a little hard."

TJ almost smiled. She knew he was trying to make

her feel good and she loved him for it. Glancing down at her mother's necklace, she began thinking of their conversation the other night. "Dad?" she asked.

"Mwess, mweetheart." It was supposed to be "Yes, sweetheart," but sometimes talking is hard when your mouth is sealed shut with yellow glue.

"You told me Mom never said a bad word about anybody."

"Mwat's mwight."

"Because she always tried to think good things about them?"

"Mwuh-huh."

"But how . . . how do you do that? I mean, think good things about people all the time?"

She waited for him to wash down his food with a big drink of a buttermilk biscuit (which might have had just a little too much buttermilk in it).

"That's a great question," he said, trying to stop his eyes from watering (thanks to the bottle of hot sauce she'd accidentally dumped into the buttermilk). "I think your mother just kept reminding herself that each of us is God's creation. And no matter how mean people may be, we all need to be loved."

"That's it?" TJ asked.

"That's it," Dad said.

"Everyone needs to be loved?" little Dorie asked. "Even famous TV stars like Hesper Breakahart?"

Dad nodded. "Even famous TV stars like Hesper Breakahart."

TJ reached up to the opal necklace around her neck. "That sounds pretty simple," she said.

"Oh, it is," Dad replied. "It's not always easy, but it is simple. Now, if you don't mind, will you pass me some more of those delicious bacon bits?"

"Actually, they're pork chops." Violet smirked.

"Right." Dad nodded. "And much juicier than last week's. You really are becoming a better cook, TJ."

But TJ barely heard. Instead, she continued feeling the necklace and thinking about her father's words.

CHAPTER NINE

Hollywood Weirdness

TIME TRAVEL LOG:
Malibu, California, November 5

Begin Transmission
Subject insists on solving problems without our
helpful claws and beaks. It is unknown if she will
succeed. It is known that thanks to Tuna's singing,
I'm losing my mind. Hopefully my hearing will be
lost first.

End Transmission

The following day on the TV set wasn't as bad as TJ
had feared.

It was worse!

She thought that by luring Herby and Tuna into the garage and locking it (she couldn't find a sound-proof birdcage) and by trying to think only good thoughts, everything would turn out fine and dandy.

(She's obviously never read any of these stories.)

For starters, she wasn't thrilled about standing around in the hot sun with 100 other cast and crew members. Actually, that wouldn't be so bad if those 100 other cast and crew members weren't all standing around staring at her.

It seems she was having a little problem saying her lines—the ones about what a great person Hesper Breakahart was. The words refused to come out of her mouth. Oh, they eventually came out, but only after a lot of coughing and gagging.

So for the thousandth time the director cried, "Cut." And for the thousandth time, he said, "Okay, let's try it again." He turned to TJ. "You were magic, babe." He was just as fake as he had been at the auditions—same fake smile, same fake words, same fake hair. "But let's try it one more time—without the bit where you throw up. Think you can do that?"

TJ nodded.

"Great, fantastic, you're beautiful." He grinned

at Hesper, cranking up his smile to ultra-fake. "You okay, babe?"

Hesper shrugged and sighed wearily, which of course meant the rest of the cast and crew shrugged and sighed wearily—after all, they couldn't disagree with their star.

"Great, fantastic, beautiful," the director said. "Okay, everybody, we'll try it again."

Everyone got into position as TJ whispered to herself, "I can say these lines. It's just make-believe. I can say them."

"Quiet on the set, please," the director shouted. "Annnnnnnd . . . ACTION!"

TJ took a breath and swallowed.

"Anytime, babe," the director whispered.

She nodded, took another breath and another swallow. Well, it was now or never.

"Oh, Hesper," she said, "you're so beautiful and talented and beautiful and rich and did I mention beautiful?" TJ couldn't believe it. She was actually saying the lines . . . and without gagging! Things were going perfect. Just one more sentence and she'd be done. Just one more sentence and—

"CUT!" Hesper shouted. "CUT, CUT, CUT!"

Immediately the director ran up to the star. "What's the matter, babe?"

"It's that cloud." Hesper squinted at the sky, which of course meant everyone else in the cast and crew squinted at the sky.

"What about it?"

"I don't want it there." She raised her perfectly tanned arm and pointed her perfectly manicured finger. "I want it moved over there."

"Babe, it's just a cloud. It's not even in the shot."

"I don't care if it's in the shot!"

"Right, but—"

"Am I or am I not the star of this series?"

"Of course you are, babe."

"Then I want that cloud over there!" Turning to the rest of the cast and crew, she yelled, "Aren't I right? Doesn't it belong over there?"

"Oh yes, yes, absolutely," everyone agreed and began pointing. "Over there. It definitely belongs over there."

Hesper turned to the director with a look of triumph. "See."

"Right, right, babe. Absolutely. What was I thinking? You heard the lady. Let's move the cloud!"

Everyone agreed and began running about, trying to figure out a way to move the cloud.

Unbelievable, TJ thought. *I finally get my lines right and now this spoiled little—*

She threw a glance to Hesper and saw the star starting to shrink.

NO, NO! I DIDN'T MEAN LITTLE! TJ desperately thought. *SHE'S NOT LITTLE! SHE'S PERFECTLY NORMAL!*

And just like that, Hesper regrew the two or three inches she had started to shrink.

Luckily, no one had noticed. Well, except for Elizabeth and her new friend, the TV Gossip Lady (who'd lost her job the night before after telling the nation she had stinky feet). Now she was trying to get rehired by finding a hot story . . . and from the way she kept her video camera pointed at TJ's every move, it was clear Elizabeth had told her exactly where she could find that story.

TJ shook her head and thought, *That Elizabeth, she can be such a snake in the—*

Elizabeth dropped to her belly.

NO, NO! TJ thought. *SHE'S NOT A SNAKE! SHE'S PERFECTLY NORMAL! SHE'S A PERFECTLY NORMAL GIRL!*

A very confused Elizabeth got up off the ground, brushed herself off, and sucked her flickering tongue into her mouth.

Think good thoughts! TJ told herself. *Think good thoughts; think good thoughts!*

And what better way to think good thoughts than to look at Chad Steel, who had left school early to stop by and watch.

Ah, Chad Steel, she thought. *My knight in shining—*

She instantly heard the creaking of Chad's clothes as they began turning into armor. *NO, NO, NO! HE'S A BOY! HE'S JUST A BOY!*

And so the battle of TJ controlling her thoughts continued . . . until, at last, the cloud moved away.

The crew slapped each other on the back, taking credit for a job well done, until the director shouted, "Okay, everyone, places please!"

The cast took their places.

"Quiet on the set!" he yelled.

Everyone grew silent.

"Annnnnnnd . . . ACTION!"

TJ swallowed and began. "Oh, Hesper, you're so beautiful and talented and beautiful and rich and did I mention—"

"CUT! CUT! CUT!" Hesper cried.

Once again the director was at her side. "What's wrong, babe?"

Hesper whined, "The tip of my nose itches. I can't possibly work with an itchy nose."

"Absolutely; you're right." Turning to the crew, he

yelled, "Can we please, PLLLLEEEEEASE bring in Ms. Breakahart's nose scratcher!"

As Hesper's official nose scratcher stepped from the crowd, it happened. Hesper leaned over and whispered into TJ's ear, "I'm going to make us stand here all day and night and *everyone's* going to blame *you.*"

TJ frowned, not understanding.

"Nobody tries to steal my boyfriend and gets away with it."

"I . . . I'm not trying to steal—"

"Of course you are," Hesper snarled. "And do you know why? Because you're such a loser, you can't find a boy of your own."

TJ felt her ears grow hot in anger. Then her cheeks. *NO!* she told herself. *NO, NO, NO! Think good thoughts; think good thoughts. . . .*

Unfortunately, Hesper wasn't finished. "This is *my* set and *my* series, and I'm going to humiliate you until you're a puddle of tears. By the time I'm done with you, everyone will know you are a total waste of human life."

That did it. Before TJ could help herself, she thought, *Listen, you big, spoiled baby—*

And before she even finished the thought, Hesper Breakahart transformed into a rather large baby (if you call 5'1" and 105 pounds *large*) with a gigantic pacifier around her neck and the world's biggest pair of Pampers around her bottom.

NO, NO, NO, I DIDN'T MEAN THAT! TJ thought. But this time she did mean it, which is why this time the giant baby remained a giant baby.

Immediately, Hesper threw herself on the ground and did what all giant, spoiled babies do best:

WAAAAAAHHHH . . .

"Get a shot of that!" Elizabeth shouted to the Gossip Lady. "See what that girl did to her!"

But TJ's anger was still boiling. As she spun around to Elizabeth, she couldn't stop herself from thinking, *You really are a snake!*

"Sssee," Elizabeth shouted as she fell to the ground. "Ssssssee what she'sssssssssss, *sssssss*, *sssssssssssssssssss* . . ." Within seconds Elizabeth was slithering around, exchanging her snakeskin boots for a snakeskin body.

Unfortunately, the Gossip Lady didn't fare much better. She'd barely focused her camera on poor Elizabeth before TJ turned on her and thought, *You gossip reporters are such vultures!*

"Ahh!" the reporter cried. "What's happening tooo *meeeee* . . . *TOOOO-MEEEEE* . . . **TOOOO-MEEEEE** . . ." (Which, of course, is the sound all vultures make, especially when sprouting feathers, growing wings, and developing breath even worse than African elephants.)

But things weren't over yet. TJ's anger was still red-hot and it didn't get any better when the director ran up to the wailing Hesper and shouted, "Babe, babe—" (well, at least he got that part right)—"what's wrong?"

WAAAĀAAHHHH . . .

Hesper *waah*-ed.

The director spun around to TJ and shouted, "What did you do to her?"

TJ started to answer. Unfortunately her mind was still working faster than her mouth. *What do you care?* she thought. *You're nothing but her puppet!*

And just like that, the director became (you guessed it) a marionette—complete with all those strings attached to his arms, hands, and feet. Strings that Baby Hesper grabbed and yanked

boing-boing-boing-ing

him up into the air and

boing-boing . . .

CRASH-ing

him onto the ground.

The good news was the director puppet was great fun for the baby and helped quiet her down. The bad news was he was starting to

boing-boing . . .

CRACK

boing-boing . . .

BREAK

into pieces all over the set.

Meanwhile, the cast and crew were in a panic,

running this way and that, screaming, "WE'RE ALL GOING TO DIE!"

Even though TJ tried to calm them down by shouting, "No, you're not! Everything will be all right!" inside, she was thinking, *You Hollywood types pretend to be so cool when you're really nothing but a bunch of fraidy-cat—*

And (you guessed it again) before she even finished the sentence, the set was overrun with a bunch of

    meow   **meow**

           meow   **meow**

      meow   **meow**

         meow   **meow**

    meow

frightened kittens.

But the part you didn't guess was that TJ's thinking didn't end there. To the phrase *fraidy-cat* she added one extra thought. It wasn't big. Just one word: *chickens*. And suddenly the entire cast and crew became a pack of fraidy-cat

meow-cluck meow-cluck-cluck meow-cluck

meow-cluck meow-cluck-cluck meow-cluck meow-cluck meow-cluck meow-cluck-cluck-cluck-cluck

chickens!

That right. As if things weren't bad enough, TJ Finkelstein had invented a brand-new species of animal. It would have been on the cover of this book but the **SPCE**—**S**ociety for the **P**revention of **C**ruelty to **E**yeballs—said it was just too creepy, so you'll have to use your imagination instead. Are you ready? Here goes . . .

Imagine a chicken covered in thick fur, with pointy little ears, cute whiskers, and a tail that swishes back and forth.

Not seeing it? Okay, try this:

A cat with an ugly orange beak, spindly legs, and giant, flapping wings.

(Now you know why they're not on the cover.)

Poor TJ. She wasn't sure whether to call the animal shelter or ask Colonel Sanders if he wanted to add something new to his menu. Either way, it wasn't the end of her little vacation to Insane-ville. Because just when she was sure things couldn't get worse, things got—well, you'll have to read ahead and see for yourself.

(By the way, do fraidy-cat chickens lay eggs?)

CHAPTER TEN

So For Those of You Keeping Score . . .

TIME TRAVEL LOG:

Malibu, California, November 5—supplemental

Begin Transmission

Subject in deep quod-quod. Fortunately, she came to her senses and realized Tuna's and my incredible genius . . . though she still doesn't get my awesome hunkiness.

End Transmission

By now you may have noticed TJ should have had a different thought when she thought what she'd thought instead of thinking what she shouldn't think when she thought what she was thinking.

> **TRANSLATION:** She was in trouble.
> (I think.)

So for those of you keeping score, we have

1 very big TV star in diapers
1 slithering best ~~friend~~ snake since forever
1 vulture with very bad breath
1 TV director literally going to pieces
100 furry chickens aka feathered cats

And if that wasn't bad enough, none of her new pals were playing nicely together. Not that you can blame them. The vulture was only doing what vultures do best by

toooo-meeeee . . . toooo-meeeee

chasing the snake all over the set for an afternoon snack.

But don't feel bad for the snake because she was doing what she does best by

SSSSSSSS . . . . SSSSSSSSSSSSSSSSSS

trying to gulp down some of those tasty fraidy-cat chicken eggs. (Well, I guess that answers the question about the eggs.)

Meanwhile the 100 fraidy-cat chickens were doing what all cats do best by

meow-cluck   meow-cluck-cluck meow-cluck meow-cluck   meow-cluck-cluck meow-cluck   meow-cluck meow-cluck meow-cluck-cluck-cluck-cluck

trying to catch one very large vulture-type bird.

All this as Baby Hesper continued

WAAₐAₐAHHHₕ-ing

and the director puppet continued to

boing-boing . . .

CLUNK

clatter . . . clatter . . . clatter

TJ stared at all of this in horror. What had she done? Worse than that, what had she *thought*? Everybody was destroying everybody else and it was all her fault! Unfortunately, there was only one thing left to do.

"TUNA!" she shouted. "HERBY!"

But Tuna and Herby were still locked in her garage . . . until TJ had a brainstorm. (Actually, it wasn't that big . . . more like a brain tropical depression. No, less than that . . . more like a brain slightly overcast day.) The point is, it wasn't much of a thought, but it was the best she had.

Guys, figure out how to get out of my garage and join me here on the set.

And just like that, the boys were circling her head

chirp-chirp-chirp-ing

and

screeeeetch, scraaaatch, scraaaaap-ing

their little hearts out.

"Hang on!" she said as she pulled the cell phone from her pocket and switched it on to hear what they were thinking.

"Wow, she's really zworked things up," Tuna thought.

Herby agreed. *"Worse than the other books."*

"I guess practice really does make perfect."

"Guys," TJ shouted, "I need your help!"

"Oh, now she decides to ask."

"Please," she said. "I'm really sorry."

"What do you think?" Tuna thought.

"I mean it. I'm really, really sorry."

"Well, if she's really, really sorry."

"Please, guys."

The robin and canary shrugged their shoulders or wings or whatever it is birds shrug and fluttered down to sit on her shoulders.

TJ was glad they didn't hold any grudges. She would have been gladder if it weren't for the 100 fraidy-cat chickens who started scampering up her legs as they realized robins and canaries are a lot easier to catch than vultures.

"HERBY!" she cried. "TUNA!"

The boys flew back into the air where it was safe—except for dodging that diving vulture, who was still trying to catch that slithering snake.

"What do I do?" TJ yelled.

"Obviously," Tuna thought, *"you must think everyone to their original selves."*

"Right!" TJ shouted as she shook off the last of the fraidy-cat chickens. "Okay, here goes!" She closed her eyes and yelled, "I think you're all really nice people!"

But when she opened her eyes, nothing had changed.

"It's not working!" she shouted.

"Because you don't really believe what you're thinking," Tuna thought.

"You're just pretending to think it, Your Dude-ness."

TJ nodded. They were right. So once again she closed her eyes and once again she yelled, "You really are really, really nice people. Really!"

She opened her eyes but there was still no change.

"You're still pretending," Tuna thought.

"What do I do?!"

Herby looked at Tuna.

Tuna looked at Herby.

And then, combining all of their 23rd-century genius, each bird gave another shrug.

TJ was lost. Big-time. There was nothing she could do. This was all her fault and there was absolutely—

"Whenever somebody got on her nerves, she tried to

think something nice about them." It was her father's voice—what she remembered him saying when he'd given her the necklace.

"But how . . . how do you do that?" TJ had asked him later at the dinner table.

"I think your mother just kept reminding herself that each of us is God's creation," he had said. *"And no matter how mean people may be, we all need to be loved."*

TJ reached up to the necklace and ran her fingers over the opal. That was it, the key: *Each of us is God's creation. . . . We all need to be loved.*

At last she had her answer. She looked down at the fraidy-cat chickens running in all directions. The truth was, most of them were just men and women trying to make a living so they could feed their families. No wonder they were afraid. How scary to know they could lose their jobs if someone like Hesper Breakahart simply decided not to like them. Scary . . . and sad.

And just like that . . . the 100 fraidy-cat chickens turned back into 100 cast and crew members, completely normal (well, except for the eggs some found in their pants).

Next, TJ glanced at the director puppet, whose wooden body lay scattered all over the ground. Poor guy. He was just trying to keep the show going by making sure the spoiled star was happy.

And just like that . . . the director became human. All his body parts came together (well, except for his fake hairpiece, which the wind kept blowing around the set).

TJ looked up to her bird buddies flying in the air. "Guys, it's working!"

"That's great," Tuna thought, *"but what about us?"*

Ignoring him, TJ looked over to the vulture, who had just caught the tail of the snake in her beak. She frowned, trying to think of something good, anything good. Unfortunately, nothing came to mind. Nothing except . . . *"Each of us is God's creation."*

And just like that . . . Elizabeth and the Gossip Lady were their old selves (well, except that the Gossip Lady was currently chewing on Elizabeth's shoe).

"What are you doing?" Elizabeth demanded.

"Sorry," the woman said, spitting it out.

"Uh, Your Dude-ness?" Herby thought from high in the air. *"What about thinking us back?"*

"Oh, sorry." She closed her eyes and thought, *"You guys really are sweet . . . though sometimes a little weird."*

And sure enough, the boys became themselves . . . though they weren't crazy about

"AuHHHH!"-ing

50 feet through the air until they

Thud-ed

incredibly hard onto some not-so-incredibly-soft ground.

Now, at last, everybody had returned to normal. Of course they were all pretty confused and eyed TJ pretty suspiciously. But at least everyone was back to themselves.

Well, almost everyone . . .

"Whew." Elizabeth scowled. "What's that smell?"

"Don't look at me," the Gossip Lady said. "I'm wearing shoes. Maybe it's that giant baby in the Pampers that needs changing."

It was true. Everyone but the

WAAaAaaHHHH-ing

Hesper had returned to normal.

Tuna leaned toward TJ. "Well, go ahead," he whispered. "Think her back."

TJ nodded. But as she stared at Hesper, all she could do was think of what a big baby the TV star was. Which is why the TV star remained . . . a big baby.

"Your Dude-ness?"

TJ frowned. "I'm trying." But nothing seemed to work.

Only then did she see Chad Steel walking toward the baby.

"Hesper?" he called out to her. "Hesper, is that you?"

Once the baby saw him, she let out an even louder

WAAaAaaHHHH

"It's okay," he said, gently trying to calm her. "Don't worry. We'll find a way to help you." At last he fixed TJ with those big blue eyes. "Is this . . ." He cleared his throat, trying to sound as kind as possible. "Are you the one who did all this?"

TJ looked down at the ground a moment, then nodded.

"So are you like an outer space alien or a witch or something?"

She shook her head and croaked a faint "No."

"Good, I'm glad. I was hoping you weren't."

TJ's heart skipped a beat. Actually, it skipped several. Actually, it might have stopped beating altogether.

He continued speaking. "Look, I don't know what's going on or how you did all this . . . but how come you changed everybody back except Hesper?"

"I . . ." But as always, TJ's words caught in her throat. "I'm not sure . . . how to do it."

Chad paused a moment, then looked at the crying baby. TJ could tell he was confused. Who wouldn't be? But she could also tell he felt terrible for Hesper. Real terrible.

Finally he turned to TJ. "You know, she really isn't such a baby—underneath all that spoiled selfishness." With a smile, he added, "Waaay underneath."

TJ tried to smile but wasn't sure she pulled it off.

He continued more sadly. "She's just . . . you know, really insecure. No one can see it, at least on the outside, but inside she's really afraid of people. Inside she thinks everybody hates her." He sighed. "And I suppose she's probably right."

"But—" TJ finally managed to clear her throat— "not you. You don't hate her."

"Maybe it's because I feel sorry for her. I don't

know. The best I can tell, I'm like her only real friend, so she sorta needs me. I mean, every person should have at least one friend, don't you think?"

TJ's eyes filled with moisture and she looked away.

"Are you okay?" he asked.

Not trusting her voice, she could only nod.

"You're not crying, are you?"

She shook her head and took a swipe at her eyes. What an incredible boy he was. And what a friend . . . at least to Hesper Breakahart.

He took a deep breath. "Anyway . . . if you wouldn't mind trying again, maybe a little harder. Something like this could ruin her career. It's really not her best look, if you know what I mean."

TJ turned back to those wonderful, sensitive blue eyes. It took a moment to catch her breath, much less restart her brain. But once she was able to think, she knew Chad was right. Everybody needs a friend. Even the Hesper Breakaharts of the world. And if Hesper was acting so creepy because she was afraid she didn't have any, then maybe she wasn't such a selfish baby after—

And just like that . . . Hesper was her old self. Her old, *spoiled* self.

"What's going on?" she demanded. "What are you all staring at? Get to work!"

Immediately the cast and crew scurried about pretending to be busy.

"And whoever's got that baby," Hesper shouted, "will you please change its diaper! It's really stinking up the . . ." She came to a stop and felt the seat of her jeans. Then, with a strange look on her face, she raced toward the nearest restroom.

"All right, everyone." The director clapped his hands. "You heard the lady. Let's try this scene again."

As everybody moved about getting ready, they were careful to keep an eye on TJ. And she was careful not to get caught as she whispered to Tuna and Herby, "Guys, they can't know all that weird stuff happened. What can we do?"

"Actually," Tuna said, "the solution doesn't lie with us. It lies with you. And it couldn't be more obvious."

"That's right," Herby said. "It couldn't be more obvious. What is it again?"

Tuna sighed. "She just has to think everyone back to the start of the day before all this craziness began. That way no one will remember a thing."

Herby turned to TJ with a nod. "Exactly."

"Nothing? No one will remember anything?" TJ asked.

"Not a thing," Tuna repeated.

She paused and looked over the crowd. It was

amazing what a terrible mess she'd made. All because she had thought the worst of people. "And you'll be able to fix that thought-broadcasting thingy so this won't happen again?"

"Absolutely," Tuna said, "now that we've returned to being human and have regained the use of our hands."

"It will work perfectly," Herby said.

TJ looked at him skeptically.

"Well, except for the usual fritzing and shorting out."

She paused another moment, then glanced at Chad. He was clearly grateful Hesper had been changed back. When he looked over to TJ and their eyes met, he gave a quiet nod of appreciation. And ever so softly, he mouthed the word *Thanks.*

She nodded in return. Seeing no other solution, TJ made her decision. She took a deep breath, closed her eyes . . . and thought everybody to the beginning of the day.

And just like that, Hesper Breakahart was standing beside her demanding, "Can we start the scene, please?"

"Absolutely, babe," the director said. "Okay, places, everybody." As the cast and crew got into position, he waved TJ over. "You all set?"

TJ nodded.

"Fantastic. Now, don't be nervous. Just make believe you've done this a thousand times before."

TJ nodded and smiled. *If he only knew,* she thought. Then, catching herself, she added, *But it's better he never does.*

"All right," the director called to the cast and crew. "Quiet on the set, please. Annnnnnnnd . . . action!"

CHAPTER ELEVEN

Mopping Up

TIME TRAVEL LOG:
Malibu, California, November 6

Begin Transmission
Subject's life has returned to normal. Well, as
normal as normal can be when surrounded by such
abnormals as us two greater-than-normal normals.
Normally speaking, that is.

End Transmission

"Hey, TJ, wait up!"

TJ stopped near the basketball courts as the
World's Greatest Breath Mint

Click-clack

CRUNCH-er

Naomi Simpletwirp and her boyfriend,
Doug-the-Allergy-King-

sniff-sniff

SNORT

Claudlooper, approached.

It was always a mystery to TJ how Doug could push up his glasses, hold Naomi's hand, and wipe his nose all at the same time. The guy definitely had talent. Maybe that's what Naomi saw in him. Whatever the reason, the fact that she never wore gloves proved it was true love.

"So why are you going home this way?" Naomi asked.

TJ threw a look to the group of guys playing basketball—particularly the one who just happened to have the bluest, most sensitive eyes in the whole world. "Oh, I don't know," she said.

Tuna, who instantly appeared floating beside her, groaned. "Unfortunately, we do."

"What's that?" Naomi asked.

"Incredibly blue," TJ said, trying to cover his words. "The ocean—it's incredibly blue." She gave Tuna an angry look.

"Right," Naomi said suspiciously, "the ocean is . . . incredibly blue."

TJ nodded and forced a smile.

"Everybody's talking about the great performance you (*sniff*) gave for Hesper's (*snort*) show yesterday," Doug said.

"Yeah," Herby sighed, "if you only knew."

"What's that?"

"If it were only true," TJ said, shooting Herby a glare.

"Oh, it's true," Doug said. He wiped his nose again, giving the back of his hand another coat of shiny sheen. "Who knows? With any luck, you'll get to be in another episode."

TJ nodded, thinking this was obviously a new definition of the word *luck*.

Naomi popped another mint into her mouth. "We're heading over to the coffee shop. You wanna come?"

TJ shook her head. "I think I'll stay here and enjoy the scenery a little longer."

"Yeah, I bet you will," Doug snickered as he looked over to Chad Steel.

Naomi responded by giving him

OoOFF!

a good jab in the gut with her elbow.

TJ pretended not to hear but felt her ears start to grow hot.

"Well, okay then," Naomi said. She and Doug started toward the coffee shop up the beach. "Maybe we'll catch you a little later."

"Yeah," TJ called after them, "later."

Once they were out of earshot, Herby muttered, "'Enjoy the scenery.' Give me a break."

"Don't you guys have someone else to haunt?" TJ asked. "Maybe fix that Swiss Army Knife or time pod or something?"

"We do have a lot to do," Tuna agreed. "But we wanted to stop by and make sure you thoroughly learned your lesson."

"My lesson?"

Herby sucked in his stomach and flexed his muscles. "About where to find the *real* scenery."

OoOFf!

This time it was Tuna's elbow that found Herby's gut.

"Actually," Tuna said, "it's the lesson about always speaking well of others."

"Oh, I learned that, all right," TJ said as she reached up to finger her mother's necklace. "I also learned to always try to think the best about them."

"Why's that?" Herby asked, still rubbing his stomach.

"Because God created everyone," TJ said. "And everyone deserves to be loved."

She'd barely spoken the words before a giant silver object filled the sky. It looked like some cheesy UFO from some cheesy sci-fi flick . . . and it was dropping toward them fast!

"What is it?" TJ cried.

No one had an answer as the UFO slowed to a stop and began hovering 100 feet over their heads. Only then did they notice what looked like 1,289 laser cannons pointed at them.

"Uh-oh," Herby said.

"Uh-oh," Tuna agreed.

They were answered by a deafening voice that roared from the craft:

"GREETINGS, ZWORK-OIDS!"

A deafening voice that sounded exactly like . . .

"BRUCE BRUISEABONE!" Tuna shouted.

"AND HE'S USING THAT STUPID ENGLISH ACCENT!" Herby yelled. "WHAT DO WE DO?"

The laser cannons adjusted slightly, taking aim, and they had their answer.

"RUN!"

The guys took off down the beach. The good news was the craft followed them and left TJ behind. The bad news was those laser cannons

zZZZzzZZap

POW!

zZZZzzZZap

SIZZLE!

zZZZzzZZAP

"Ouch!"

worked pretty good.

The boys fought back with their own weapons. Unfortunately, all they had was their

"AuGHHHHHHH!"

hysterical screaming.

Luckily, the guys and the UFO were totally invisible to Chad and the other players on the basketball court. Unluckily, the *ZZZZZZZAP-ing*, *SIZZLE-ing,* and *"AUGHHHHH!"-ing* were very visible—er, audible.

Chad had the ball and stopped playing. Everyone had turned to check out the sounds . . . and to stare at TJ. Of course, they saw nothing except TJ dropping her head and examining the tops of her tennis shoes.

Gradually, the screaming and vaporizing faded until Trent Tauntalot yelled, "C'mon, let's play!"

But Chad was still curious about the sounds . . . and TJ.

"C'mon, Steel!" Trent slapped the ball out of Chad's hands and it rolled across the sand, stopping directly at TJ's feet.

(Insert **gulp** here.)

TJ stooped and clumsily picked it up. When she rose, there was Chad Steel standing directly in front of her.

(Insert **double gulp** here.)

"Thanks," he said.

She nodded but had no idea what he said. (It's hard hearing anything when your heart is doing a jackhammer imitation in your ears.)

He held out his hands.

She stared at them, confused. What did he want? Was she supposed to take them? hold them? run into his arms and be his forever?

He cleared his throat. "Uh, the ball?"

TJ looked down and saw she was still holding it.

"Hey, Romeo," Trent shouted, "lay a fat juicy one on the chick and let's get back to the game!"

TJ's eyes widened in embarrassment as her cheeks started to burn.

"Don't worry about him," Chad said. "He gets that way whenever he's losing."

"Steel!"

"And all the other times, too." Chad flashed her that killer smile of his.

TJ might have smiled. (It's hard knowing if you're smiling when you're trying to breathe.)

He motioned toward her hands. "The ball?"

She looked down to see she was *still* holding it. Talk about embarrassing. She quickly threw it at him—a little too hard and a little too fast, considering they were 2½ feet apart.

Still, Chad managed to catch it. "Thanks," he said, checking for broken fingers, then looking at her quizzically.

If TJ's cheeks were burning before, it was time to call the fire department now.

He started toward the court, then faced her again. "I didn't get a chance to tell you how good you were yesterday—doing the TV show, I mean."

It was definitely time for TJ to recheck the tops of her shoes.

"No, I'm serious," he said. "I thought you were great."

Somehow she found the strength to look up . . . and there was that killer smile again.

"If you ask me, Hesper better be careful." His smile became a grin. "She just might have some competition."

TJ said nothing. She thought nothing . . . well, except *Don't pass out . . . don't pass out . . . don't pass out . . .*

"Steel!"

"Gotta go." With that, he turned and trotted toward the court.

TJ mumbled something that she hoped was in English and might have sounded like "Me too." Finally she found the strength to turn and start walking up the beach toward home (though it really wasn't walking since technically your feet are supposed to touch the ground).

Later that night, TJ might have eaten dinner—she wasn't sure.

And she might have done her homework—she wasn't sure of that, either.

But she was sure of one thing: she would never forget Chad's parting words. The words that kept her awake all that night as she stared at the ceiling. The words that made her heart flutter and her stomach feel like she'd just swallowed a herd of butterflies. . . .

"Hesper better be careful. She just might have some competition."

Turn the page for a sneak peek at

Ho-Ho-Nooo!

the next wacky adventure in the TJ and
the Time Stumblers series by Bill Myers.

CHAPTER ONE

Beginnings . . .

TIME TRAVEL LOG:

Malibu, California, December 18

Begin Transmission:
Subject is not fond of video games. I, on the other hand (spit-spit), am not fond of geraniums.

End Transmission

"Fire proton torpedoes!" Captain Tuna shouted.

"Aye-aye, Captain!" the ever-loyal (and always dim-witted) Lieutenant Herby called back. But before Herby could reach over and push the button labeled

WARNING: Push only if you want to blow stuff up and make a real cool mess!

their spaceship was struck by a powerful explosion. The craft lurched violently to the left and was suddenly filled with the sounds of

"Row, row, row your boat—"

"Oh no!" Captain Tuna shouted.
"Oh what?" Lieutenant Herby shouted back.
"He hit us with the Stupid Song Bomb!"

"—gently down the stream."

Not only was the entire spacecraft filled with the silly stupidity, but so were the brains of the entire crew (i.e., Tuna and Herby—well, actually, only Tuna for sure, since medical science has yet to determine if Herby has a brain).

"Merrily, merrily, merrily, merrily—"

"Augh!" Captain Tuna cried, grabbing his head in agony.

"Groovy!" Lieutenant Herby said, tapping his foot in ecstasy.

"Raise the deflector shields!" Captain Tuna shouted.

But Herby was too busy singing along to hear the orders.

Another explosion hit, throwing the craft to the right.

*"Twinkle, twinkle, little star,
How I wonder what you—"*

Captain Tuna leaped from his chair and staggered toward the control panel. "Must . . . stop . . . the . . . music!"

But before he arrived, they were hit again.

*"Jack and Jill went up the hill
to fetch a pail of—"*

And again.

*"Here we go round the mulberry bush,
the mulberry bush,*

the—"

Just when Tuna was about to lose his mind (leaving the spacecraft with a grand total of zero minds), the singing was interrupted by an even worse sound.

"Greetings, zwork-oids!"

Tuna spun around and gasped. There, on the giant viewing screen, was the vilest of all villains, Bruce Bruiseabone. He stood on the bridge of his own spaceship, laughing his creepy

"moo-hoo-ha-ha-hee-hee-hee"

laugh.

Captain Tuna watched in horror as the villainous man put his villainous hands on his villainous hips and spoke (what else?) villainously.

"And so, my mini-micro-minds, we meet again."

"What do you want from us, you fiendish fiend?" Tuna shouted.

"I want you to hand over the keys to your spacecraft."

"Never!"

"What?" Bruce shouted back. "You dare challenge me, the most villainous of all villains?"

"That's right!" Tuna yelled defiantly.

"We're the heroes of this story," Herby explained, "and heroes always win!"

"Have it your way." Bruce turned to one of his crew members and shouted, "Fire torpedoes!"

Once again the ship lurched, and Tuna's brain (and whatever there was of Herby's) was filled with

"The itSy-bitSy spider crawled up the water—"

"AUGH!" Tuna *augh*-ed.

"Shh," Herby *shh*-ed. "This is my favorite part."

"Down came the rain and waShed the spider—"

"Not only will you hand over your keys," Bruce shouted again, "but you will give me those giant foam dice hanging from your rearview mirror."

"Oh no!" Tuna cried. "Not the foam dice!"

"Guys?" a female voice suddenly called from below. Another bomb struck:

"Are you sleeping, are you sleeping? Brother John? Brother—?"

"Guys!" The female creature stuck her head up through the spaceship's floor. She had dark hair, wore glasses, and was incredibly smoot (at least according to Herby—well, all right, according to Tuna, too.) "What are you two doing?" she shouted.

Immediately Tuna grabbed his Swiss Army Knife (sold at 23rd-century time-travel stores everywhere) and closed the blade. The holographic video game disappeared. No more spacecraft, no more Bruce Bruiseabone, and no more irritating music. The fancy starship had changed back into a dusty attic.

"Hey," Herby complained, "I was really getting into that song."

He got a frown from the female—a seventh-grade girl better known as Thelma Jean Finkelstein (TJ to her friends—all four of them, if you count her goldfish and hamster). She'd just moved from Missouri to Malibu, California (which explains why she had only four friends). If that wasn't bad enough, she had become the history project of Herby and Tuna, a couple of goofball teenagers from the 23rd century who'd traveled back in time to do a school report on her. Apparently she was going to grow up to become somebody important (if she survived junior high).

Unfortunately, the guys' time-travel pod had run out of fuel and they were stuck here.

Unfortunatelier (don't try that word in English class), TJ was the only one who could see them.

Unfortunateliest (the same goes for that word), people could still hear them.

"I told you," she whispered, "no video games after nine o'clock."

"We were just practicing." Herby flipped aside his surfer bangs and flexed his muscles. (He was always flexing his muscles to try to impress TJ.)

Tuna explained, "We need to be prepared in case Bruce Bruiseabone reappears."

"I thought he went back to the 23rd century," TJ said.

"He did," Herby agreed as he spotted a tiny fly buzzing the room.

Tuna continued. "However, there's no telling when he'll show up again to torment us."

"Or—" Herby lowered his voice and watched the fly buzz toward the attic window—"what form he'll take when he does."

"Listen, guys," TJ said. "You can practice all you want when I'm at school and nobody's home."

"How can we protect you at school if we're practicing at home?" Tuna asked.

"My point exactly," TJ said. "I've told you a hundred times I don't want you following me." She paused to watch Herby tiptoe toward the window.

"Understood," Tuna said. "However—"

"AₕHHHHₕₕ!"

He was interrupted by the sound of Herby leaping at the fly. But Herby's leaper was a little lame and he was unable to stop at the window. Instead, he sort of

CRAₛₕ! BREAK!

tinkle-tinkle-tinkle

leaped through the glass and

Poll, Poll, roll

"Ouch! OUCH! ouch!"

tumbled down the roof until he

THUD

"Oooff!"

landed in the flower bed.

Tuna and TJ raced to the window.

"Herby, are you all right?" TJ cried.

"Wuaff mwabom!" Herby replied (which is the best anyone can reply with a mouthful of geraniums).

"What?"

"Mwi maid (*spit-spit*) false alarm," he finally shouted. He held out his hand and revealed one very squashed fly. "It wasn't Bruce after all!"

"Excellent news," Tuna shouted.

Of course it would have been more excellent if TJ's father wasn't shouting from downstairs, "What's going on up there? TJ, are you okay?"

Luckily, Tuna had an answer for everything. (The answer was usually wrong, but he always had one.) Without a word, he pulled open the Reverse Beam Blade of his Swiss Army Knife and

RaaÓapha . . .
Reeeepha . . . RiÏÏipha . . .

BoinG-oing-oing-oing-oing!

everything

"!FFOoo"

DUHT

that had happened

"!hcuO !hCuO !hcuO"
llor, llor, llor

was put into

elknit-elknit-elknit

!kaeRB !HSARC

reverse, until

"!HHHHHHHA"

Herby was back in the attic having the conversation about not following TJ to school.

Not that TJ was surprised. It was just another average, run-of-the-mill evening for TJ Finkelstein and her time stumblers.

* * * * *

TJ climbed down the attic steps and headed toward her bedroom. As she passed Violet's door, she saw that her middle sister still had the lights on. No surprise there. Violet always had her lights on. How else could she read 50 books a day, be president of every club in her school, and become dictator of the world before she was sixteen?

TJ pushed open the door to see Violet standing on a ladder. She was writing numbers on a big thermometer chart that stretched up to the ceiling.

"What are you doing?" TJ asked.

Violet answered without turning. "I'm checking to see how much more money I need to earn for Daddy's gift."

"Gift?" TJ asked. "For what?"

"Christmas. It's only 6 days, 2 hours, 6 minutes, and 46 seconds from now." (Violet liked to be precise.)

"No way!" TJ cried in alarm. "It can't be!"

"You're right." Violet rechecked her watch. "It is now 6 days, 2 hours, 6 minutes, and 41 seconds." (See what I mean?)

TJ couldn't believe it. She'd been so caught up in all her junior-high migraine makers that she hadn't even noticed it was December. It would have helped to have a few clues . . . like maybe a little less sunshine or the temperature dropping below 70 degrees. Still, if she'd been paying attention, she'd have noticed that the beach babes had changed from SPF 69 to SPF 41.

"I'm getting him an 82-inch plasma TV and installing it right in his bedroom," Violet said snootily. Violet didn't try to sound snooty; it just came naturally. "What are you getting him?"

"Something better than that," TJ said. TJ didn't try to compete with her sister . . . it just came naturally.

"Yeah?" Violet asked. "Like what?"

"Like . . . well, uh . . . it's a surprise!"

"Right," Violet snorted and went back to coloring her money thermometer.

"What? You don't think I can give Daddy a better gift than you?" TJ asked.

"Actually," Violet said, "I don't think you can do anything better than me."

TJ could feel her insides churning. She knew it would do no good to argue with her sister. Violet always thought she was right. To make matters worse, Violet always *was* right. (Well, except that one time when she thought she was wrong.) But she couldn't help saying, "Oh yeah?"

Violet gave no answer.

TJ pushed up her glasses and repeated, "Oh yeah?"

"Listen," Violet said, "don't take it personally. It's in our DNA. I got all of Mom's and Dad's brains and you got all of . . . all of . . . Well, I'm sure you got something. I mean it's not like you were adopted." She hesitated, then turned to TJ. "Were you?"

If TJ was mad before, she was outraged now. So outraged that she returned to her favorite argument. "Oh yeah?"

Violet sighed. "Haven't we already had this discussion?"

TJ wanted to fire back with a classy put-down, but somehow she knew another "oh yeah" wouldn't do the trick.

"Guys?"

They both turned to see their youngest sister,

Dorie, standing in the doorway. She was as cute as a button and almost as small.

"Can I borrow some markers?"

"Hey, Squid," TJ said. "Why are you out of bed?"

"I'm getting Daddy his Christmas gift."

"You too?" TJ groaned.

"Uh-huh," Dorie said. "I'm making him a tie clasp." Her face beamed with excitement. "I already found the clothespin. Now I just need to color it with markers."

"You're giving Dad a clothespin for Christmas?" TJ asked.

Dorie shook her head. "No. I'm giving him a clothespin *colored with markers* for Christmas."

"I see." TJ smiled. She always smiled when she talked with Dorie. Of course she tried to hide it. After all, Dorie was a younger sister, and younger sisters are supposed to irritate older sisters. (It's like a law or something.) So TJ just tousled Dorie's hair and said, "Let's head to my room to see if I have any."

"Yippee!" Dorie said as she skipped into the hallway.

But even as they headed toward her room, TJ's mind raced back to Dad. She had to get him something. Granted, she had no money, but somehow the gift had to be bigger and better than Violet ever dreamed.

Unfortunately, some dreams turn into nightmares—especially with help from the 23rd century.

Read all six wacky adventures in the

TJ and the TIME STUMBLERS series

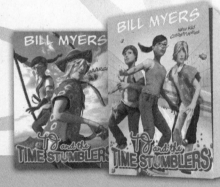

#1 New Kid Catastrophes—*Available Now*

#2 Aaaargh!!!—*Available Now*

#3 Oops!—*Available Now*

#4 Ho-Ho-Nooo!—*Available Now*

#5 *Available Spring 2012*

#6 *Available Spring 2012*

RED ROCK MYSTERIES

BRYCE AND ASHLEY TIMBERLINE are normal 13-year-old twins, except for one thing—they discover action-packed mystery wherever they go. Wanting to get to the bottom of any mystery, these twins find themselves on a nonstop search for truth.

CP0140

Would you like Bill Myers

(author of TJ and the Time Stumblers series)

to visit your school?

Send him an e-mail:

Bill@billmyers.com